Hussy
By Selena Kitt

eXcessica publishing

Hussy © 2013 by Selena Kitt

Excessica LLC
P.O. Box 127
Alpena, MI 49707

To order additional copies of this book, contact:
books@excessica.com
www.excessica.com

Cover art © 2013 Humble Nation
First Edition "Falling Down" 2009

Chapter One

"You can't wear that!"

Lindsey glared at him, inwardly seething, her little fists clenched at her sides. *I'll wear any damned thing I please!* She gritted her teeth against the words, something in her daring them to come out.

"You want me to change, *Daddy?*" Her voice dripped saccharine, her eyes veiled.

"If you ever want to leave this house, I suggest you put on something decent!" His gaze swept over the orange tube top and white satin shorts and she saw his eyes darken with something other than disapproval.

"Fine." *Asshole! Who do you think you are? My father? Feh!* Lindsey stormed back upstairs, grabbing her biggest purse, the floppy crocheted one with the flap on top. She wiggled her shorts off and shoved them in the bag, and after pulling the top over her head, she shoved that in, too. She found a pair of Capri pants and a t-shirt, yanking them quickly on and bounding back down the stairs again.

"Better, *Daddy?*" She made sure her voice remained high and light, but her eyes bored holes into his skull.

His eyes hesitated at her breasts, no bra to contain them, her nipples pointing skyward. Finally, he sighed, "Fine. What time should I tell your mother you'll be back?"

Whenever I want to be back.

"Midnight."

She slipped her sandals on and headed out the door, slinging her purse over her shoulder. In the garden behind the house, she stripped down to nothing in the beginning dusk, shoving her clothes into her purse. The white satin shorts and orange tube top were liberated from her oversized bag, and Lindsey wiggled them past her slim, naked hips, the shorts barely covering her bottom, the tube top simply accentuating the hardness of her nipples.

Mission completed, she saw their neighbor, old Mr. Finn, standing with a garden hose in his hand, his eyes wide, his mouth open. Lindsey gave him a wave as she passed the fence.

"Hey, Mr. Finn, how's it hangin'?"

He mumbled something and the hose jerked in his hand, sending water spewing skyward before he caught it again. She didn't stop to hear what he had to say. It was a half a mile walk, and she was already running late.

* * * *

Someone's dad built the tree fort in one of the tall trees at the edge of the subdivision. It was secluded, down a well-worn path, fifteen feet off the ground with just a railing around the edge, the boards nailed to the side of the tree the only way up or down. Lindsey heard them before she saw them, someone's radio blasting not quite loud enough for the surrounding neighbors to call the cops.

"Coming up!" She put her foot on the first board nailed into the trunk of the tree, and began to scale the side. There were three of them sitting up on a blanket spread over the platform, passing a bottle around. Brian, the one she'd met walking through the aisle at the grocery store earlier that day, gave her a wave and patted the platform next to him.

"Getting late." He draped his arm around her slight shoulders as she settled back against the railing. "Thought you might not show."

"My stepdad." Her tone was enough of an explanation. "I have to be home by midnight."

"Midnight? What can you do by midnight?!" One of the other guys snorted—he was cute, too, although not as cute as Brian. His hair was curly and almost as dark as his eyes. Lindsey took the bottle from him, meeting his eyes as she drank a swig, the alcohol making her eyes water before she passed it on to the third guy. He was smaller than the other two, his blonde hair almost as long as hers.

"Guess we just have to start earlier," Lindsey gasped, her throat still burning. The dark-haired guy gave her an appreciative look at her comeback, and they all laughed. That made her feel warmer than the alcohol.

They introduced themselves and passed the bottle again. The dark-haired guy was Ralph, a senior from Xavier. The quiet blonde said his name was Wayne. He looked older than the other two. Brian had already made his introductions earlier that day, when he'd invited her to this little party. She knew him by sight anyway, from the halls at school. He was a senior, like she was, at Chippewa.

"Hot enough for ya?" Ralph peeled off his t-shirt and hung it over the railing. "Christ, this summer is gonna be a bitch, and I have to spend it roofing with my uncle."

"Sun's going down," Wayne remarked and Lindsey glanced at him as he tipped the bottle toward her. "Should get a little cooler."

"Hey, dude, you were supposed to get me in on that gig." Brian's hand moved over her bare shoulder and Lindsey settled in closer, feeling a warm glow in the pit of her stomach. "It's gotta be better than stocking cans at the Sav-Way."

"Yeah." Ralph shrugged. He was across from Lindsey, leaning back and stretching both arms out to rest on the railing. "Still workin' on it."

A long silence stretched into the coming night. Lindsey felt the coolness of the evening settling on her damp skin. They were all peeking glances at her—she felt Brian's eyes on her top, Wayne's moving over her legs, and Ralph's were focused between them. Her shorts were pressed between her pussy lips and she felt the seam riding there every time she moved.

"Oh I love this song!" She reached over Wayne to turn up the radio and felt him startle at the weight of her on him, her hand pressing into the meat of his thigh. Giving him a smile of apology, she eased her way off, and he smiled back.

"Gimme a hand." She turned to Brian. He did, and she used the leverage to pull herself to standing. The tree fort seemed even higher when she could see the ground, so she closed her eyes, standing in the middle of the platform and swaying to the music.

She kicked off her sandals, dancing barefoot, letting the pulse of the music move her body, feeling them watching, even though she couldn't see them. She let herself go, undulating and swaying, her head back, her arms up, her long, blonde hair falling to her waist as she arched and rocked to the rhythm. All the while, she felt their eyes on her.

"Nice show..." Ralph's eyes followed her as she collapsed, breathless, in the middle of the platform at the end of the song.

"I have to pee," Lindsey announced. "Where should I go?"

Brian waved his hand. "We just pee off the side."

"Oh." She looked around the circle and met each of their eyes, and then grinned. "I can give it a shot."

Standing up, Lindsey walked over to the railing, peering over the side at the fifteen foot drop below. The sun was really beginning to set now, spreading a pink hue over everything.

"I don't think I have the right equipment for this," she said with a little laugh, looking back at them over her shoulder. "Maybe I should just climb down..."

"We can help you," Ralph offered. He was standing next to her before she could say yes or no, his head jerking in Brian's direction, calling him over. "Here, let us hold you."

Lindsey looked up at him with wide eyes as he grasped her upper arm and Brian did the same on the other side. "Are you serious?"

"Sure." Ralph gave her a small smile. "Just pull your shorts down and go. We'll hold you."

They flanked her on either side as she slipped her shorts down over her hips, her eyes meeting Wayne's. He was still sitting in his spot, tipping up the bottle and watching.

"Don't drop me," she warned, grabbing onto them, her fingers hooking onto the waistband of their jeans. "You promise?"

"We got you," Brian assured her as she sank into a modified sitting position, her bare ass hanging over the railing, her thighs resting there, her feet not touching the platform. "Just go."

"I don't know if I can..." She laughed and then closed her eyes and bit her lip, concentrating hard. *Ahhh, there!* She let go in a gush, the sound of her release raining down on the underbrush below. The rush faded to a trickle and then stopped.

"Okay." She glanced between them. They were both looking down at her and she smiled. "Guess I have to drip dry."

The guys lifted her, pulling her easily back onto the platform. Her shorts puddled at her feet and she saw Wayne staring between her legs.

"Nice pussy," he remarked before tipping the bottle back again. Lindsey swallowed hard, seeing his eyes darken.

"You got a better view than we do." Ralph gave a short laugh, leaning forward to take a look. Lindsey flushed. "Oooo shaved...nice!"

"Yeah?" Brian leaned forward to look, too. "Oh man...yeah...nice..."

"Hey!" She tried to reach for her shorts, but their grip on her arms restrained her. "Come on..."

"Bet it's nice and smooth." Ralph's breath was hot against her cheek. "Can I feel?"

"Whoa, wait a minute..." she said, but his hand cupped her mound, rubbing his fingers roughly over her skin. "Guys... this..."

"Mmm nice and smooth," Ralph confirmed, making her gasp and struggle between them when he slid a finger between her lips. "Nice and wet, too..."

"Let me feel." Brian's hand replaced his friend's and Lindsey's eyes met Wayne's. He was watching them closely and now he had a hand cupped over a bulge in his jeans. "Oh baby, that's such a sweet little pussy...she's just begging to be fucked..." Lindsey's heart raced as she stood, caught between them, their fingers digging in tighter into her upper arms every time she moved.

"I've wanted to fuck you since I saw you coming down my aisle," Brian said into her ear, his finger sliding deeper up inside of her. "Those tight short shorts, and that skimpy little top..."

"Yeah, let's see what's under there," Wayne called, and Lindsey glanced at him long enough to see him unzipping his jeans and reaching a hand in. "I want to see her tits."

"Hey!" she cried when Ralph pulled the orange tube-top down to her waist, revealing the slight mounds of her breast with their pointed nipples.

"Just a handful," Wayne scoffed. She flushed at his words and when she looked at him, she saw his hand moving inside of his jeans. "Nice nips, though."

"Guys...wait, I think I should go..." She struggled to pull her top back up. Brian's fingers were still buried in her pussy, and both boys had a hand on her upper arm, gripping her between them, but Ralph's other hand was free, and he grabbed her wrist, keeping her from covering herself.

"I don't think so." Ralph shoved the tube top down even further, over her tiny waist. It caught at her hips, where Brian's hand worked slowly between her legs. "I think you need to stay right here a while. Don't you think so, guys?"

They all nodded and muttered their agreement, and Lindsey looked between them, eyes wide. All she could say was, "Please!" as Ralph pressed her to her knees on the blanket. Brian's fingers were gone from her pussy, but it didn't matter, because he bent her forward to her hands and knees and spread her lips to finger her again from behind. Her tube top was still caught around her waist, a bright band of color on her pale flesh in the fading light of the day.

"Oh god," she whimpered, pulling the blanket into her fists as she heard the sound of a zipper near her ear. Behind her, Brian's fingers slipped up and down her slit, opening it a little. The air felt cool between her legs, her bottom up, completely exposed to him. "Please, please, please..." she begged.

"Shhhhhhh." The words came from the other side, into her other ear, and she looked through the curtain of her hair to see Wayne stretching out beside her. His hand moved lightly over her shoulder and back, trailing his fingers over her skin. "It's okay..."

"Don't." She shook her head, feeling Brian pressing something hard against her pussy. "Please!"

"Let's give that pretty mouth something else to do!" Ralph's hand moved in her hair, turning her head his way, and then his cock was in her mouth, pressing past the initial resistance of her lips, searching out the soft palate at the back of her throat with his heat.

"Oh fuck!" Brian groaned as he slid his cock between her smooth, wet pussy lips, grabbing her slim hips in his hands and pulling, pushing himself in deeper. "Oh yeah, that's a hot little cunt!"

"Is she tight?" Wayne's voice came from Lindsey's other side, but she couldn't see him. She was too busy trying not to gag as Ralph thrust himself deeper into her mouth. There was a hand cupping and squeezing her breast, and she thought it must be Wayne, fingering her nipples, back and forth between the two as Brian began to fuck her.

"Oh yeahhhh," Brian groaned, pulling her back into the saddle of his hips. "Like a glove...god!"

Lindsey moaned around Ralph's cock, his hand going to the back of her head, shoving himself so deep she couldn't do anything but choke on his length. The fingers moved between her nipples, twisting and tugging, and she gasped for air when Ralph slid himself out of her mouth completely for a moment.

"Oh baby, yeah, that's it!" Brian shoved himself into her now, faster and harder, the sound of their bodies slapping together echoing around them through the trees. "Take that dick!"

Ralph slapped her cheeks with the wet length of him, making her gasp and squirm. He pumped it slowly from base to tip, teasing the head around her lips.

"That's good..." Wayne's voice was near her other ear, and she felt something against her thigh, a fast motion, the press of something spongy and wet, and knew he must be masturbating, rubbing himself against her leg as he watched her get fucked. "You like that cock, baby? I can't wait to shove mine into that wet little hole..."

"Me, first," Ralph insisted, grabbing her head and, using her hair to pull it back, shoving his cock back into her mouth. Lindsey groaned again, gagging as he thrust himself in deep. He held himself there, forcing the head into her throat until she could barely breathe.

"Ohhh baby, yeah," Brian moaned, his cock plunging hot and fast into her pussy. "I'm gonna come!"

"Don't come inside, man!" Ralph insisted. "I don't want no sloppy seconds."

"Make her swallow it," Wayne urged.

Brian groaned as he pulled out and there were hands on her, flipping her over on the blanket. Brian's jeans were in a pile behind her and he straddled her face, pressing his cock between her lips. He gave a few good thrusts and Lindsey's nails dug into his thighs, straining against him as she felt hands pressing her legs open and back.

"Ohhh yeah, swallow it, baby, swallow my cum!" he moaned, rocking into her throat. His cock exploded with his climax, sending hot, white jets streaming over her tongue. Lindsey whimpered but could do no more, feeling Ralph's cock sliding between her swollen pussy lips as she swallowed Brian's cum. He kept rocking in and out of her mouth, moaning softly, even after she had swallowed it all.

"Hey, gimme some of that." Wayne nudged Brian and she saw him looming above her, his cock in hand, outlined by the trees above in the fading sunlight.

With a sigh, Brian rolled off her and leaned back against the railing while Wayne straddled her face, pressing his cock to her lips. She felt her top bunched up around her ribs now and she caught only a brief sight of Ralph rutting between her legs, his eyes closed, head back. His cock, thick and swollen, moved deep inside of her.

Lindsey moaned and tried to turn her head when Wayne's cock met her lips, but his fingers gripped her jaw, turning her toward the meaty head and slipping it into her mouth. Lindsey couldn't do anything but take it. Luckily, Wayne was nowhere near as big as Ralph or Brian, and he could shove himself to the back of her throat without making her gag.

"Come on, man," Brian urged and she saw him out of the corner of her eye, slipping his pants on.

"She's so tight!" Ralph groaned and Lindsey felt him gripping her thighs, spreading them wider as he leaned his weight into her.

"Yeah, I know." Brian grinned as Wayne rocked in and out of Lindsey's mouth, groaning all the while.

Ralph's fingers dug into her flesh and he gave a deep thrust, shuddering against her. "I'm gonna come!"

"Hey, no fair!" Brian cried. "Not inside!"

"Fuck!" Ralph groaned, pulling his cock out of her mid-stream, his cum christening her exposed clit. The next wave was strong and shot across her belly, leaving a thick rope of white stuff from navel to pussy. The next shot right against her pussy again, the hot pulse making Lindsey moan and squirm under Wayne's weight.

"My turn!" Wayne moved down and settled himself between her thighs as Ralph moved aside, still panting and looking dazed.

"Please," Lindsey gasped, trying to sit up as Wayne aimed his cock between her legs.

"Oh, no you don't." Ralph hauled his pants up with one hand. "We all get a turn, that's only fair."

"Oh god!" Lindsey cried as he grabbed one of her arms and held it down while Brian grabbed the other.

"Hurry, Wayne," Brian urged, his eyes moving over Lindsey's face. She looked down and saw Wayne looking at her pussy, his fingers moving over her lips, Ralph's cum making her slick. "Come on, put it in! Fuck her!"

"Okay, okay." Wayne bit his lip, his eyes closing the moment he slipped his cock head between her lips. "Ohhhhhhhh fuck!"

"Yeah," Brian grinned at Ralph over Lindsey's head. "I know."

Lindsey looked back and forth between them, pleading with her eyes. "Please, you guys... I..."

"Be a good girl," Ralph murmured, watching Wayne press her legs back and thrust his hips into her. "It'll be over soon."

Brian chuckled, seeing the look on Wayne's face. "Very soon."

"Oh god, oh god, oh god!" Wayne whispered, his breath coming hard and fast as he fucked her. She felt him swelling inside of her, as if he were going to burst. "Baby, that's so good...oh god..."

Lindsey squirmed against their hold, the motion of her hips rocking Wayne between her legs. He gasped, his eyes flying open, and grabbed her thighs, arching against her with a loud groan.

"Hey!" Brian cried, watching as Wayne shuddered between Lindsey's legs, filling her with his cum. She felt it beginning to leak out of her pussy, so much of it! It was running down the crack of her ass. "No fair!"

"Sorry!" Wayne gasped, panting and still gripping her thighs. "I couldn't help it!"

Lindsey rolled to her belly with a groan, seeing her shorts and grabbing them. She pulled her top quickly up and tugged her shorts on, which only accentuated the sticky mess between her legs. She didn't look at any of them, and they didn't say anything to her, either. She just picked up her bag and shoved her shoes in, swinging herself down and feeling for the ladder with her bare toes.

"See you in school on Monday!" Brian called down the ladder as she reached the bottom. She didn't reply, starting down the path toward home, but she heard him say something like, "What did I tell you about her?"

When Lindsey snuck behind the house, she noted her mother's car beside her stepfather's. In the garden again, she stripped down to nothing, this time under cover of darkness. Her shorts were soaking wet with their cum and she lifted the silky material to her face, inhaling deeply. These were the shorts that got Brian's attention in the first place, she remembered, smiling. They hadn't ever failed her.

Her pussy was still dripping, swollen. She leaned her back against the cool side of the house, her bare feet spread wide, and touched herself, remembering. Pressing her shorts to her nose, she could smell them all as she rubbed at her throbbing clit with her thumb, her fingers moving in and out of her aching pussy. She could still feel their cocks, in her pussy, in her mouth.

"'That's a hot little cunt!'" she whispered, rubbing faster, the slippery sounds of her pussy filling the garden. "'Take that dick!'" She found the crotch of her shorts, the smell strong there, the material wet. She pressed it to her tongue, tasting cum and her own juices. "'Be a good girl... oh... oh yes... oh...'" Her climax was coming, and she worked for it, sucking at the material now, her words muffled. "'Swallow my cum!'"

Her back arched and she quivered against the side of the house, burying her hand deep into her pussy as she came, her muscles spasming again and again. The image of them taking her, fucking her, wanting her, all those cocks... she trembled and leaned against the side of the house for support, the memory making her weak and breathless.

Lindsey inhaled the smell of them again before shoving the shorts into her purse and taking out the clothes she had worn for her stepfather's benefit. When she slipped through the side door, her feet dirty and bare, she heard them talking in the living room. Trying to sneak up the back stairs, she gasped when she heard her stepfather's voice behind her.

"You're home early."

"Yeah," Lindsey agreed with a shrug. "So?"

"You stay out of trouble?" He frowned. His eyes were moving over her, like they always did.

"Of course," she replied innocently, continuing up the stairs to her room. She dug into her purse and found her shorts. She fingered the material with a smile, remembering, knowing she would have to hand-wash them again, so her mother wouldn't discover, before next time.

Chapter Two

"Why don't you stay in the car?" Her mother asked, but the tone wasn't a question, it was a demand. "I'm just going to pick up your father's dry cleaning."

"He's not my father." Lindsey pulled at her tube top—this one was red, but she was wearing the shorts, white satin, no panties. Her stepfather was out of town for business and hadn't been around to put the kibosh on her clothing choices. It was the outfit—she was sure her mother didn't want anyone to see it.

Her mother sighed. "I'll leave the keys. You can listen to the radio."

"Fine." Lindsey turned it up full blast, closing her eyes, leaning the seat back and putting her feet up on the dashboard. The air was on in the car, but the sun was still warm on her bare legs. The seam of her shorts rubbed between her thighs and it felt good, making her squirm in her seat. She couldn't wait to get home from "running errands." She wanted to call Brian and see if he could meet at the tree fort, because she was so horny she could barely stand it.

She thought she might have dozed off. A different song was playing when she leaned up and peeked out the window to see if she could see her mother.

"What the hell is she doing?" Lindsey grabbed the keys out of the ignition and her purse off the floor, storming barefoot across the parking lot. The bells over the door tinkled as she swept it open, finding her mother standing at the counter talking to the owner.

"They've lost your father's blue blazer." Her mother gave a frustrated sigh.

"No lose!" The man was clearly foreign, trying to explain something to her mother in two different languages.

"Whatever!" Lindsey waved her mother's words away. "And he's not my father." She turned to the kid behind the counter. He was about her age, kinda cute, she noted, and most definitely staring at her bare midriff and long legs. "I have to pee. Do you have a bathroom?"

"In the back," the kid offered. Lindsey padded after him, leaving her mother and the owner to work things out. He pulled open a door that said: *Employees Only.*

"Gee, I must be special, huh?" Lindsey flashed him a smile as she turned on the light and tossed her purse on the floor.

"We don't usually let customers—" the kid's voice trailed off and he stood open-mouthed as he watched her pull her shorts down and sit on the toilet to pee.

"What's the matter?" Lindsey pulled toilet paper off the roll and wiped. "Never seen a girl pee before?"

He shook his head, eyes wide and staring between her legs as she pulled up her shorts and flushed the toilet. Lindsey washed her hands at the sink, glancing at him in the mirror. He was still standing in the doorway, transfixed. Plucking her purse from the floor, Lindsey shuffled through and found some lip gloss. She leaned way over the sink to the mirror, up on her tiptoes, rolling the tip of the tube over her lips.

"Uh... I guess I should get back up front..." He cleared his throat, moving to shut the door. His eyes were still between her legs and Lindsey could feel the pull in the seam of her shorts and knew they were riding up between her pussy lips. It all felt too good to stop.

"Or..." Lindsey smacked her lips together, tossing the lip gloss into her purse and turning to face him with a smile. She slid up slowly onto the sink and swung her bare feet. "You could come in, shut the door, and fuck my brains out."

"I… uh…" His hesitation told her everything she needed to know. Lindsey hopped off the sink and came toward him, reaching past him to shut the door, forcing him fully into the room. His eyes were still glazed, stunned, and he licked his lips as he looked down at her. "I don't even know you."

"I'm Lindsey." She cupped the bulge she knew would be in his jeans. "Who are you?"

"Fred…" His eyes widened even more the moment her hand began to rub at his stiff cock.

"Now we know each other." Lindsey dropped to her knees and unzipped his pants. "Let's fuck."

"Oh my god," he groaned when she freed his cock and put it into her mouth. She sucked him completely hard, but he bounced back up the moment she let him go, and so she turned around and bent over the sink.

"You want to pull down my shorts?" She looked back over her shoulder at him.

"Yeah," he said hoarsely, glancing toward the door with his cock in his hand. "Shit, I could get fired for this."

Lindsey grinned, meeting his eyes in the mirror. "And my mother's out there waiting for me. Aren't we just so bad?"

His hands moved over the silky material, rubbing it between her legs. Lindsey bit her lip and arched against his probing fingers.

"Come on." She reached between her legs and pulled her shorts aside to show him her shaved pussy. "Just put it in and fuck me."

He cocked his head to peer between her legs, his hand moving up and down his shaft. Lindsey sighed, reaching her hand back and spreading her lips with two fingers.

"Here, Fred!" She whistled, as if she were calling a dog, sliding one of her fingers into her pussy. "Right here, boy."

The head of his cock touched her pussy, nudging her finger aside. Their eyes met in the mirror and he frowned, swallowing hard.

"I..." he started, and then cleared his throat.

"Let me guess." She wiggled back against his cock head, feeling the tip easing its way between her lips. "You've never done this before?"

He shook his dark head, looking down to where his cock was disappearing into her flesh. "Got close, a couple times, with a few girls, but..."

"Well, just think of the story you'll have to tell all your friends." Lindsey went up on her toes and arched her back, feeling more of his shaft slip into her. "How for your very first time, you fucked some hot little slut in the bathroom at work..."

Fred gasped as Lindsey reached around for his thigh, pulling him completely into her pussy and squeezing him there.

"Fuck me, Fred!" She grabbed onto the edge of the sink, her eyes bright as they met his startled ones in the mirror. "Fuck me until you come inside my tight little cunt—and you better hurry, before your boss or my mommy decide to come looking for us."

"Condoms?" Fred squeaked, and Lindsey used her not inconsiderable pussy muscles to squeeze his cock hard, making him jerk inside her and eliciting a low groan from his lips.

"To hell with condoms, Fred." She rolled her eyes, rocking her hips back against him, moving his cock in and out of her wetness. "I can't get pregnant."

"But..." His hands went to her rolling hips, his eyes looking down between them, where his cock was spreading her wide.

"Worried about diseases, Fred?" She sighed, slapping her ass back into him, making him gasp and clutch her ass. "Let's just live fucking dangerously, what do you say?"

"Oh hell!" His eyes closed as his hips began to move.

"That's right." Lindsey pulled her top down and squeezed her nipples. "Fuck me good, baby. Give me that hard cock."

His movements were jerky and unsure and Lindsey sighed again, working her hips back into his. Her pussy was swollen and soaking wet, but she knew it would be over far too soon for her to come. He was already panting and gripping her ass so hard his knuckles were white.

"When a girl tells you to fuck her..." Lindsey reached back for his thigh again, driving him deep inside. "She means it. Now, fuck me!"

He groaned and shoved her into the sink with his next thrust.

"Yeah!" She spread wider. "Come on, Freddie, do it hard!"

Finally, he gave her what she wanted, his hips bucking her against the sink, burying his cock in her to the hilt again and again. Wouldn't be long now, she knew, seeing his eyes in the mirror. He was watching her tits bounce through half-closed eyes as he fucked her, and she was glad she had pulled down her top.

"Oh god!' he moaned, leaning forward onto her as he came. She felt the surge and swell of him, a thick pulse inside her tight, wet hole. She bit her lip and squeezed him, slowly, rhythmically, making him gasp and squirm against her as she milked him for all she was worth. She wanted every last drop of his cum.

"That's a good Freddie." She tilted her hips forward and felt him slip out of her. She turned and patted him lightly on his flushed cheek. He leaned back against the wall for support, gasping for breath, his eyes glazed. "Now you can say that you fucked a girl...how about that?"

Lindsey pulled up her top and grabbed her purse. Yanking the door open, she peeked around the corner. Her mother was *still* haggling with the owner! Adjusting her shorts, she strode back out front, past them both.

"I'll be in the car," she told her mother on the way by, straight-arming the door.

When she got into the passenger's side, she scrunched down in her seat, keeping an eye on the dry cleaner's. The crotch of her shorts was soaked from her own juices and Fred's cum. She rubbed the material between her swollen lips, her fingers pressing them into the wetness.

Putting her feet up on the dashboard, Lindsey pulled her shorts aside and plunged her fingers into her pussy. Fred's cum was thick and copious, leaking out of her hole. She scooped out as much of it as she could and licked it off her fingers first, moaning at the taste and smell of it and rubbing the seam of her shorts over her clit with her other hand as she did.

"My first cherry," she murmured with a laugh, remembering, still delighted at how surprised he had been. She wanted to take her shorts off, to lick them clean, but didn't dare, with her mother about to come out of the store. Instead, she pulled them aside and fingered her sopping pussy, her thumb moving over her aching clit, taking herself closer and closer to the edge.

"Oh yeah, fuck me hard, baby," she moaned softly, looking out the window, still watching for her mother with half-closed eyes. "Use that little cunt!"

She was nearing climax when she saw him out of the corner of her eye. There was a man standing next to the passenger's side window, looking down at her as she played with herself. His eyes were wide and he was carrying a bucket of Kentucky Fried Chicken in his hands, clearly just returning to his car.

Lindsey grinned up at him, grabbing her top and pulling it down, too, as she rubbed herself.

"You want a show, baby?" She moved her hand aside so he could see her pussy completely as she circled her clit. The look on his face, something caught between shock and deep lust, sent her flying over the edge, and she came so hard she had to grit her teeth against it, squeezing her eyes shut as her body bucked and rolled on the seat.

Breathing hard, she opened her eyes to see his hand cupping a bulge in his jeans. She grinned, wondering if there was time…but then she saw her mother hurrying across the parking lot in her business suit and heels, carrying dry cleaning bags over her shoulder.

Lindsey gave the man a wink, pulling her top back up and adjusting her shorts, putting her feet back on the floor. He was still staring at her as she licked her fingers clean.

"Hi, Mom," she said when the driver's side door opened. She heard her mother saying something to the man, but couldn't quite hear it. "What was that all about?"

"Didn't you see that man staring at you?" Her mother frowned, holding her hand out for the keys. Lindsey dug through her purse for them, glancing out the window to see the man pulling quickly away.

"No," Lindsey replied innocently, handing her mother the keys. "Was he?"

"You young girls." Her mother sighed, starting the car. "So unaware…"

Lindsey hid her smile, closing her eyes and leaning her head back. She couldn't help wiggling a little against the seat, and knew there might even be a wet spot there on her stepfather's BMW upholstery.

"Did they find his blazer?" Lindsey didn't open her eyes.

"Yes," her mother replied. "Finally! Thank goodness, because you know how your father gets. It was that young kid who finally found it. I gave him a little extra tip."

"You too?" Lindsey murmured, still smiling.

She could feel her mother's silence and Lindsey quickly covered, opening her eyes and saying, "He's not my father. I wish you would quit saying that."

"Oh Lindsey." Her mother sighed. "Why do you have to be so difficult?"

"Gee, Mom, I don't know…" Lindsey frowned, glaring out the window. "Maybe I was just born that way."

Chapter Three

She changed in the bathroom at school. She kept her blouse on, but she unbuttoned the top and bottom three buttons, leaving only the middle two fastened and tying the shirt tails up high around her ribs. Her denim shorts got shoved into her purse and the white satin ones went on over her bare bottom. She snapped the elastic band and turned to look at herself over her shoulder in the full length mirror with a satisfied grin. *That should do it.* When she bent forward, the shorts rode up between her thighs, exposing the swell of her behind quite nicely. *That should do for at least a three-day vacation!*

Her eyes bright, Lindsey put her hands on her knees, bit her lip, and looked back over her shoulder, whispering, "I've been a very bad girl!" to the mirror. Then she grinned and slapped her own ass hard enough to leave a red handprint there before grabbing her purse and heading to her first hour class. The halls were practically empty, since the first bell had already rung, and her clogs made a clatter on the tile floor as she hustled around the corner.

She had English first hour and had no doubt about the reaction she was going to get wearing her shorts or the lecture that would ensue about the school's dress code. Grinning in anticipation, Lindsey tugged her shorts up a little higher between her legs, feeling the hot pulse beating there already. The computer lab was just a few doors away from her first hour, a few of the screens still on, glowing blue in the darkened room and Lindsey slowed to peer inside.

Computers was the only class she had ever cared about or earned an "A" in. She knew Mr. Ryan had a prep period this hour, but she turned on the light and called his name anyway. No one answered. She stared at one of the screens for a moment, considering, and then shut the light off again, slipping into the room and closing the door.

She had quickly learned how to bypass the school's Internet security. It was a simple parental control device, easily diverted with a few backdoor tricks. Lindsey's fingers paused on the keyboard at the image search engine, and then typed: "hot fuck." Twenty full-color thumbnail images popped up, most of them depicting a wet cunt getting good and fucked with a nice, thick cock. She felt her own pussy beginning to throb as she scanned through the photos.

Ohhhh, there's one—a wet, shaved pussy with a nice hard cock pressing against the round center of her ass. Lindsey squirmed in her seat, clicking the picture to enlarge it. *God, that's a nice cock!* She wiggled in her seat, feeling the heat between her thighs increasing as she clicked on the "video" search option. Pictures were nice, but live action? Oh, so much better...

"Yes!" she whispered, leaning forward to get a better view of the action. His cock was incredible—big and thick, with a fat, ridged head. She licked her lips, watching as the spongy head pressed against the tight ring of the girl's asshole. The blonde's hands were holding her cheeks open for him. Searching for the sound, Lindsey found the dial and turned it up, hearing the blonde moan, "Ohhhh god, wait! It's too big—I can't take it!"

"Yes you can..." Lindsey encouraged the girl on the screen, slipping her hand down under her shorts. Her pussy was already wet and swollen in anticipation, and she parted her lips, rubbing her little clit with one finger as she watched the blonde try to take more of the cock in her ass.

"Please, god, I can't!" The blonde on the screen moaned, but she lifted her ass in the air and spread wider as he thrust forward, the head of his cock slipping into her tight hole. Lindsey moaned, her finger moving faster, and then the clip ended.

"Damn!" Using her left hand, she pointed the mouse to the next "free clip" and clicked. She tickled her clit with her finger as she waited for it to download. Biting her lip, she slipped her hand under her blouse, tweaking her nipple with a shiver as the movie clip started to play. The blonde was really getting pounded in this one, moaning loudly into the bed.

"Oh yeah!" Lindsey rubbed faster, watching through half-closed eyed. "Fuck that ass..." She had a sudden urge to be filled, and slipped her fingers down, plunging them into her wetness. Nowhere near as good as a cock, but it still felt good. Fingering herself faster, she strummed her clit with her thumb, spreading her legs wide in the chair.

"Ooo yeah, come in my ass!" The blonde moaned and Lindsey moaned, too, feeling her own asshole twitch at the thought. She worked her pussy harder, her breath a fast pant. God, she wanted to come so bad...

"Lindsey!"

Mr. Ryan flipped on the light switch, standing wide-eyed in the doorway. She sighed, slipping her fingers out of her pussy. Mr. Ryan's mouth worked, but no sound came out. His face turned another shade of red when she slid her hand out of her shorts. With a small smile, she licked her fingers, waiting for him to say something.

"Lindsey..." He cleared his throat, running a hand through his dark hair. "I think you'd better go to the principal's office."

"I thought you'd never ask." She grabbed her backpack and followed him down the hall. The principal's office was nearly empty and Lindsey sat across from a dark-skinned black man who looked like he was on his way to a parade. His white uniform practically glowed next to the darkness of his skin.

"Wait here!" Mr. Ryan directed her with a frown, knocking on Mr. Miller's door.

"I'm not going anywhere." Lindsey shrugged, pulling her knees up to chest and resting her chin on them. She glanced over at the guy sitting across from her and noticed him looking at her. Smiling, she slid her legs back down, slipping down in the chair and letting her legs fall open a little. She saw his eyebrows go up, and he lifted his gaze to her face.

"You're a very pretty girl."

She shrugged. "Yeah? So?"

He adjusted his white hat, still meeting her eyes. "So you don't have to do that to get attention."

Lindsey frowned, snapping her legs together and sitting straight up. "Do what?"

"You know what."

"What are you all dressed up for—a parade or something?" Lindsey squinted at him and saw he was wearing a name tag: *Lieutenant Zachary Davis.*

"I'm a recruiter."

"For what?" Lindsey snorted, looking him up and down. Even the man's shoes were white! "The Pillsbury Dough Boy?!"

He raised an eyebrow in her direction. "The U.S. Navy."

"So you're... what... a sailor?"

"On a nuclear submarine, but yes." He cocked his head at her. "Do you have any interest in the Navy?"

She rolled her eyes. "Only if we're at war."

"We are."

"Yeah, well... not here we're not."

"So what *are* you interested in...Lindsey?"

He'd obviously been paying attention. She leaned forward, putting her elbows on her knees and her chin in her hands. "Sex... Zach."

"Is that all?"

"No..." She glanced over at the secretary, who was rifling through papers at her desk, but clearly listening to them. "I also like pina coladas and getting caught in the rain."

He laughed. "But are you into health food?"

"Are you kidding me?" Lindsey smiled back. "I live on Twinkies and Taco Bell."

"Kraft Macaroni and Cheese, here."

She grinned back at him. "I love that stuff."

"What else do you love?"

"Hm..." Lindsey fidgeted. "I love dogs... but I'm not allowed to have one."

"How come?"

"My parents." She sighed.

"Are you a senior?"

"Yes." Pulling a pack of gum out of her bag, she slid a stick out with her teeth.

"Eighteen?"

She offered him a piece. "Yep."

He shook his head. "So you'll be out on your own soon and you can make up your own mind about whether or not you want a dog."

"I can't wait!" She crumpled the wrapper and slid the stick of gum between her teeth.

He sat forward a little. "So... what else do you love?"

"You're weird."

He shrugged. "Just a question."

The silence stretched for a moment, and then Lindsey said softly, "Snow."

"What else?"

"Argyle socks...and you know those little machines that sell those toys in grocery stores?" She snapped her gum. He nodded. "I love those. I still have to put a quarter in one every time I go."

He laughed. "What else?

"Twizzlers." She smiled. "And the blues."

He looked surprised for the first time. "Who's your favorite?"

"I like Stevie Ray Vaughan and Eric Clapton... old stuff."

He snorted. "Old, eh?"

"My favorite, lately, though, is Kenny Wayne Shepard."

"Really?"

"Really."

"Well that's a strange coincidence..." His grin grew wider. "I happen to have tickets to Kenny Wayne Shepard playing at the Palladium on Friday."

"You do not!"

"I actually do."

"Really?"

"Want to go?"

"Are you serious?"

"Would the Pillsbury Doughboy kid you?"

"Lindsey!" It was Mr. Ryan calling from the principal's office. She'd almost forgotten about him!

"Here's my number." Lindsey grabbed her crumpled gum wrapper and opened it, scribbling furiously. "Call me. I have to go get paddled."

"Excuse me?" Zach raised his eyebrows as she grabbed her backpack.

"Lindsey!" It was Mr. Miller this time, his face already red.

"I've been a bad girl." She smirked, nudging Zach's shoulder with her hip as she passed. She didn't look back, but she had the strong feeling he was watching her ass wiggle in her shorts as she walked toward where Mr. Miller and Mr. Ryan were flanking the principal's office door.

"Lindsey—" Mr. Miller shook his head as he waved her in.

"I know, I know." She snapped her gum, throwing her backpack on the floor and flopping into the chair next to his desk. "Save the lecture, Dad."

Mr. Miller nodded to Mr. Ryan. "Thanks for bringing her down, Jim." Mr. Ryan sighed, pulling the door closed as he left.

"So what do I get today?" She grinned at him, turning sideways a little in the chair and throwing one leg over the side. "Please tell me it's a spanking along with my ticket to ride the ol' suspension train!"

"You're a very difficult girl, Lindsey." Mr. Miller cleared his throat as he sat in his chair, shaking his salt and pepper head and straightening his tie.

"I know." She fixed him with her gaze as her hand slid down between her legs, pulling her shorts aside. "That's why you like me so much."

"Hey..." His eyes focused between her legs as she spread her lips, showing him pink. She was still glistening wet from touching herself in the computer room and her pussy ached.

"Oh Mr. Miller..." She slid two fingers into her wetness, pulling them out and smearing them over her lips. "I've been so, so bad. I deserve everything you can give me..." Lindsey stood and leaned over to whisper into his ear. "And I mean...*everything.*" Her still-sticky hand slipped over the crotch of his trousers, feeling his erection. He was hard, and had probably been that way since Mr. Ryan came into his office.

"Come on, Mr. Principal." Lindsey turned and bent over his desk, lifting her ass in the air. "You know I deserve it."

"Please!" Mr. Miller stood, glancing out the window and turning the blinds closed. He passed the door and pushed the button on it, locking it. She smiled, resting her cheek on his blotter with a happy sigh. "You really...need to stop. You are going to get in trouble with more than just me, one of these days."

"I can only hope." She felt his hand moving over the satiny softness of her shorts as he stepped in behind her. Closing her eyes, she spread her thighs a little wider, her pussy aching. She could barely wait for him to touch her—but it didn't take long. He yanked her shorts down to her knees, his hand coming down hard against her behind.

"What were you looking at while you were touching yourself, Lindsey?" His hand met her ass again and she whimpered and sighed.

"Nice big fat cocks." She arched, lifting her ass up for him.

"You're so bad." He smacked her again and she gasped, feeling his fingers probing her slit. "My god...you're soaking wet!"

"Can't help it." She tried to squeeze his fingers, pull them deeper inside of her. "I soooo want to be fucked."

"Do you?" His fingers slid in deeper and she moaned softly. "You want a big, fat cock shoved up here?"

"Yes." Lindsey shivered, her nipples hard against the desk. "But yours will have to do today."

"You little bitch!" His hand came down so hard on her ass that she yelped, tears stinging her eyes. She heard him unzipping, adjusting as he slipped the head of his cock between her swollen lips. He grabbed her hips, sinking himself deep into her pussy. Biting her lip, she tried not to smile in triumph and hid her face in her arms, whimpering instead.

"Mr. Miller!" Her pussy throbbed around his dick—god she wanted something bigger. She hadn't been kidding. He was average, and all right, but her pussy wanted so much more! What he lacked in size he was just going to have to make up in roughness.

"Let's see how you like that," he growled, thrusting hard into her—but nowhere near hard enough. Lindsey slid her hand between her legs, finding the aching button of her clit. One finger, back and forth, as he fucked her. That was good. Oh yes, that was very good. She shivered, her face flushing with pleasure.

"Is that all you got, Mr. Miller?" She taunted him as he rocked into her, grunting.

"You little slut," he whispered, his fingers gripping her slender hips.

"Am I?"

He drove forward hard, slamming her into the desk. "You nasty, dirty, fucking little whore!"

"Oooo yeah." Lindsey panted, squirming to keep her hand down between her thighs, rubbing her clit. "You tell me, Mr. Miller. You make that bad girl learn her lesson."

"Fuck!" He groaned, slamming into her harder, the slick slap of their flesh filling the room. Lindsey smiled dreamily, wondering if the secretary could hear them.

"That's right, Principal Miller." She closed her eyes, panting, her finger pushing her clit closer and closer toward climax. "Fuck! Fuck! Fuck! Can you fuck me harder, old man?"

"Goddamnit!" He slammed into her, fucking her forward on the desk. His hand came down over her ass, slapping her hard. "Shut up you little whore!"

"Yeah!" Lindsey wiggled under the weight and thrust of him. "You tell that bad girl!"

"I said..." He smacked her ass again. "Keep..." SMACK "Your..." SMACK "Mouth..." SMACK "Shut!" SMACK.

"Make me!" She gasped, grabbing the edge of his desk to keep from slipping as he pounded into her.

"I'll make you, all right." He grabbed her by the hair, pulling her back as he sat in his desk chair, keeping her seated right on his cock as he yanked her into his lap. He ground his hips up into her flesh, making her grip the sides of his chair. His fist tightened in her hair and he shoved her off his lap onto the floor. Tears sprung to her eyes as he jerked her head forward by her hair, forcing her lips to his cock. "Let's keep that nasty little mouth busy, what do you say?"

She didn't say anything—just tucked her gum to the side, took his cock between her lips, and sucked, slipping her fingers down to rub her clit while she did. He groaned, thrusting deep into her throat. He was nowhere too big to handle—the perfect suckable size, really—and she devoured him, her throat working, tears still leaking out of the corners of her bleary eyes.

"You're gonna swallow my cum, you fucking little slut!"

Her pussy throbbed at his words and she shoved her fingers up inside, fucking herself as she let him use her mouth. She was so close, and the feel of him swelling, the low grunting noises he made as he arched into her throat, pushed her closer and closer to the edge.

"Take it!" He gagged her with his cock, shooting cum so far back into her throat she had to struggle not to choke on it. Lindsey closed her eyes and swallowed, nudging her clit the last little bit toward her own climax. It shuddered through her as she licked the head of him, moaning and teasing the last bit of hot, white stuff from the tip.

She licked her lips, watching him struggle to pull up his pants. He stood to zip up, glancing down at her with a sigh. "You're going home, you know."

"Yep." She wiped her mouth with the back of her hand and stood, hitching up her shorts and sitting in the chair next to his desk again. "What am I getting suspended for today?"

He sat at his desk, pulling out the yellow preprinted pad that he wrote suspensions up on. Stopping with his pen poised above it, he cocked his head at her. "Fighting?"

"I can live with that." She snapped her gum. It tasted like his cum

"Three days." He tore the slip off and handed it to her. "Please try to behave yourself when you come back."

She grinned, shoving the slip into her backpack. "I'll try." Out in the lobby, the secretary gave her a dirty look, but Lindsey didn't pay any attention. The recruiter—Zach—was gone. Her stomach gave a little disappointed lurch, but then she remembered that he had her number.

He'll call.

Of course he would. Who wouldn't?

Chapter Four

The look on her stepfather's face when Zach came to pick her up would have made the whole night worth it, even if the rest of it hadn't gone as well as it did. Lindsey wasn't quite ready, and he was early—something she hadn't planned for at all. The doorbell rang just as she was tucking the tail ends of her sheer black lace blouse into her blue jean miniskirt—ends she would later tie up to expose her midriff, after she was out of the house, of course. When she heard her stepfather say, "I'll get it," Lindsey bolted for the stairs.

"That's okay, it's for me!" Her high heels clattered on the linoleum as she slid into the kitchen, grabbing her purse from the table and surprising her mother standing at the sink doing the dinner dishes. Lindsey knew she was going to be too late, and she was. Her stepfather was saying something about the Watchtower, and then she heard Zach say her name.

"I'll be home by curfew." Lindsey edged by her stepfather, smiling at Zach who stood tall in the porch light. No navy whites tonight—just jeans and a soft gray shirt.

"Lindsey? Is everything—" Her mother paused at the doorway, the dish towel she was drying her hands with stopping as she saw Zach standing on the porch. "Oh. Hello."

"Hello, Mrs. Anderson." Zach gave her what Lindsey would call a parent-placating smile. He'd obviously been taking notes when she talked to him on the phone earlier. "I'm taking Lindsey over to the Palladium to see Kenny Wayne Shepard. We'll be back no later than one."

Lindsey saw her parents exchange uneasy glances. She rolled her eyes, knowing they were entirely too politically correct to object, but that she would hear all about it later. "Yes, that's right, I'm going on a date with a nee-gro." She turned her face up to Zach, whose eyebrows raised slightly at her words. "This is the new millennium, okay? Just remember it could be worse—he could be from another planet or something."

"How do you know I'm not?" Zach was laughing. She could feel it when she pressed back against him, urging him down the steps with her body. Her stepfather's face was twisted between fear and rage, and she rather liked the look—not that she hadn't seen it before or anything. She grabbed Zach's hand, and noticed how it swallowed her own as she pulled him toward the car parked on the curb.

"Nice ride." She laughed out loud when he opened the passenger side of the black Camaro for her, glancing back and waving at her parents, still standing shell-shocked in the doorway. "You don't have to lay it on *that* thick! They're not going to like you, no matter what you do."

Lindsey tossed her purse in and followed it, flipping down the visor and putting on lip gloss as Zach went around to his side. The car smelled like oranges and sandalwood, and was absolutely spotless. He put the key in the ignition and started the car. Cold air blew over her face. When he pulled his seatbelt over, he glanced at her.

"Strap in." He nodded toward her belt.

Lindsey made a face, rubbing her full, glossy lips together. "I live dangerously."

"Not with me, you don't." Zach reached over her for the seatbelt. His body was warm, and his breath sweet, she noticed, as he clicked her belt into place.

"I thought a Navy boy would be a little more adventurous!" she scoffed, flipping the visor up as he put the car into gear. Her parents were still standing in the doorway. She wondered for a moment what they were saying—but really, she already knew. It thrilled her.

"Gotta draw a line somewhere." Zach pulled slowly away from the house, glancing in his rearview mirror. "So, tell me—what percentage of you decided to go out with me tonight based on the fact that I'm black?"

Lindsey shook her head, giving him a sly smile as she fished a pack of gum out of her purse. "Don't flatter yourself. It was the Shepard tickets that hooked me from the start. The black thing was just a nice bonus."

"And here I thought it was my witty charm and incredibly good looks." He snorted, flashing a bright smile.

"They didn't hurt ya." She winked as she crumpled the stick of gum into her mouth, wadding the wrapper and putting it in the little bag hanging from the cigarette lighter.

He glanced over at her as she pulled her shirt out of her skirt. "Neither did yours."

"Gotta accentuate the positive." Lindsey unbuttoned the bottom of her black lace shirt, tying the ends up tight under her little breasts, making them look fuller. Her bra was black under the sheer blouse and she considered taking it off and stowing it in her purse, but thought that might be too risqué, even for the Palladium. "So what do you think?"

Zach's eyes moved over her as she turned to him, holding out her arms as if to say, "taa-daa!" He shook his head, smiling. "Isn't that skirt a little long for you?"

She tugged at the hem, which didn't come to her slim mid-thigh. "Are you kidding?"

"Well, if those shorts you were wearing when I met you are any indication of your usual taste in clothes..."

She grinned. "Yeah, well... those are my 'come-fuck-me' shorts."

"Is that so?" Zach slowed the car to a stop at a red light, turning to look at her more fully. "So since you're not wearing them tonight...?"

"Oh, don't worry." Lindsey moved toward him in her seat. "You'll get compensated well for the tickets, I promise. This might not be as short, but it *is* easier access... see?" She put her knee up, flashing him a view of her sheer black panties.

"Is that why you think I asked you out?"

She smirked. "Why else? I'm not stupid."

"Do all your dates go quid pro quo?" Zach frowned as Lindsey swung her legs forward again.

"More like quim pro quo." She gave a short, sharp laugh, putting the pack of gum back in her purse. "Oh... did you want some?" He shook his head, his eyes on hers in the dimness. Behind them a car horn honked and Lindsey glanced up, noticing the light had turned green. "Um... I think you can... ya know, go?"

Zach sighed, pulling away from the light, his eyes back on the road. "I want you to know that I didn't ask you out to have sex with you."

The silence that filled the car made Lindsey feel like she couldn't breathe. She wanted to open the window and stick her head out. Instead, she snapped her gum and pressed her warm forehead to the cool glass, watching the buildings whiz by. He didn't say anything else, and she had the feeling she was supposed to respond, but she didn't know how.

"You really want to know why I asked you to come with me tonight?" His eyes flicked over to her—she felt his gaze but didn't turn. Instead, she fogged the glass further with her breath, drawing the outline of a face sticking its tongue out, and didn't answer him. "Because you still put money in those little machines when you go into the grocery store."

She laughed—she couldn't help it. "You're weird."

"We're here." Zach parked and pocketed his keys. "Still wanna go in?"

"Why wouldn't I?" She made a face, wrinkling her nose at him. "This is Kenny Wayne Shepard we're talking about!"

"Yeah, okay." He grinned. "Come on, let's go."

She took his hand as they worked their way through the crowd, and he smiled down at her, giving her fingers a squeeze. The bald guy who took their ticket stub raised a studded eyebrow at her skirt, or lack thereof, giving her a wink as she edged through the turnstile. Zach saw the exchange and stepped quickly through the gate, taking her hand again and leading her into the venue.

"You want anything?" He nodded toward the concessions and Lindsey shook her head, so they went down the stairs toward the stage.

"How close are we?" They just kept getting nearer and nearer to the stage and Lindsey glanced back, amazed at the number of seats behind them.

Zach checked the tickets. "Front row, nearly center."

"You're kidding me!" Her jaw dropped and she gripped his hand in hers. "They must have cost you a fortune!"

He shrugged, showing the tickets to a security guard before steering her down the front row. "They were worth it."

Lindsey couldn't believe how close they were and she turned to Zach, feeling his warmth as they sat, their thighs brushing. She knew her intuition was right, even before she asked the question. "You didn't have these tickets when you asked me out, did you?"

"No." He grinned and winked. "But I do now."

"Last minute, front row center seats…" She gave a low whistle. Then she frowned up at him, her eyes narrowing. "And you're telling me you didn't ask me out for sex?"

"Yep." He squeezed her hand again, his eyes on hers. His gaze made her feel warm, and every time he looked at her like that, it felt like something broke open in her chest. "That's what I'm telling you."

"Why should I believe you?"

"Why shouldn't you?"

Lindsey's eyes rolled. "I can think of about a million reasons."

"Can you think of one reason to trust me?"

She thought of the way he looked at her, how he was with her parents, and what he said tonight in the car. "Maybe."

"Hang onto that one." He squeezed her hand again and smiled.

In spite of what past experience had taught her, that's just what she did.

* * * *

Zach turned down the radio, talking over the whistle of the wind coming in through the t-tops that Lindsey had insisted he take off on the way home. Her hands were dancing in the breeze, her body still swaying to the music.

"Do you have I.D. on you?" He nudged her, getting her full attention.

"I'm not twenty-one," she reminded him and then grinned. "But I think I still have a fake I.D. in my wallet from last year that says I am."

He shook his head, smiling. "No—real I.D. Something that says you're eighteen?"

"Driver's license do?" She fished her purse off the floor.

"Yep." He took a sharp right turn, away from the direction of her house. She smiled, shaking her head. In spite of what he'd said, she was pretty sure they were headed somewhere private. During the concert, he had looked at her the way all guys do, with the heat of lust in his eyes when she ground her hips back against him as she danced. She had felt his response against her behind, in the way he gripped her hips, and she loved it.

But she thought she'd at least play along. "Why do you ask?"

"I want to show you something." He steered the car down a long, curving road. There were no houses and not even much foliage exposed by the low headlights sweeping around a turn.

"I bet you do." She couldn't help her smile, and felt a familiar warmth in her lower belly. She didn't mind that they were going somewhere—she'd been a little disappointed when he claimed he didn't want to have sex.

He smiled back, shaking his head. "It's not what you think."

"Uh-huh." She tossed her gum out the window and found her wallet in her little purse, taking out her I.D. "Is this what you wanted?"

"Thanks." He took her license and slid it above the visor, using one hand to steer while he dug into his back jean pocket for his wallet. Lindsey frowned, seeing a sign flash by on her right that she just missed reading. She didn't miss the next one though: *Air National Guard Base.*

"Uhhhh…" Her belly felt even tighter now, and she swallowed hard. "Where are we going?"

"You'll see." Zach stopped at a white, well-lit booth with a long crossbar in front, keeping cars from entering without stopping first.

Lindsey stared, wide-eyed, at the gun strapped to the man's hip as he leaned his uniformed head down to the window. "How can I help you tonight?"

Zach handed their I.D.s over. "Visiting a friend. Colonel Pullman."

The uniformed guard looked at their I.D.s one at a time, and then leaned in to take a look at Lindsey. She felt his eyes moving over her in the darkness, something she would usually relish, but tonight she found it disquieting.

"All right, lieutenant." The man handed their I.D.s back with a nod, writing something on a clipboard. "Have a good night."

"Thanks. You, too." Zach waited for the crossbar to go up, and then edged the car slowly forward.

"We're visiting a friend of yours?" Lindsey frowned, craning her neck back to look at the guard.

She had goose bumps on her arms in spite of the warmth of the night.

"Not really." He shrugged, turning the car down a side road that ran next to a tall fence topped with high, barbed wire. "Just an excuse."

"Where are we?" Lindsey leaned forward, trying to see into the darkness past the reach of the headlights. There wasn't much to see, just a bunch of small, blue lights, close to the ground.

"You'll see." Zach smiled over at her, steering the car around a curve to the right. The ground sloped upward here, and he pulled off the road itself onto the grass, parking there. She smiled as he turned the key off, listening to the engine ticking as it cooled. It was so quiet she could hear crickets chirping somewhere in the darkness.

"Pretty." She breathed deep, stretching her hands up through the open top of the car, looking up at the stars. "Is this what you wanted to show me?"

"Almost."

She smiled, sliding as close to him as she could with the gearshift between them. "Am I getting warmer?"

"Actually, no." He grinned, his teeth gleaming. She slid her hand up his thigh, leaning into his shoulder. "But I am."

"Good." She kissed his neck, the soft spot right under his ear, licking in little circles. Her fingers danced over the zipper of his jeans, just lightly, feeling for a response, some sign of encouragement.

"Not warm enough in here for you already, huh?" Zach swallowed and she felt it against her lips as she kissed her way into the dark hollow of his throat.

"Nowhere near, to tell you the truth." Lindsey breathed, trying to move closer, but she couldn't because of the gear shift, so she settled for leaning over, one hand on each of his denim-clad thighs. Their eyes met briefly before she kissed him, moaning against the softness of his mouth, the tenderness of his lips on hers. His hand moved slowly through her hair, tilting her head sideways as he sought her tongue with his.

She had been kissed a hundred times, but this was different. Something thrummed through her, and she knew her own warning system well enough. That part of her wanted to bolt out of the car and never look back—but another part of her wanted even more of him. The latter won out, and she let the kiss deepen, twining her tongue with his, feeling the spread of his hand against her lower back as he tried to press her closer.

She felt a low rumble in her belly, as if the whole car were shaking, and she gasped into his mouth as he shifted her across the console, pulling her into his lap. She felt his response clearly enough now, throbbing against her behind. He moaned into her mouth when she wiggled there, wrapping her slender arms around his neck and giving herself over to his lust.

It was then that she realized the tremor running through her was real, the feeling growing to sound in her ears as they fumbled together in the little seat. She gasped, her eyes opening in surprise to meet his as the thunder grew, vibrating the gearshift against her thigh.

"Zach!" She clutched him, turning to look out the windshield, her eyes wide. "What is it?"

"This is what I wanted to show you." He said the words against her hair, pulling her hips into him snugly. "Watch."

The sound crackled like a fire in the distance, something roaring in the night. It was too dark to see much, but a light grew brighter amidst the small blue ones on the flat ground a little ways below. The sound grew, too, the force and power of it making the whole car tremble. She clung to him, not even realizing it, her mouth dry and a heat growing in her middle.

It wasn't until the fire lit behind the F-16 that she realized what she was seeing. The plane barreled toward them like a rocket then, the sound making Lindsey cover her ears and cry out. It was coming right for them! She turned her face to hide it in Zach's shoulder and felt him shaking with silent laughter.

"It's okay, baby." The term of endearment softened her and she looked up at his bright eyes in the dimness. "I wouldn't let anything hurt you, I promise. Just watch."

Lindsey gasped, looking up through the t-tops as the plane passed high overhead, gaining altitude fast, the sound still so loud it shook her to the core, the afterburner a streak of fire behind the plane for a moment before fading to a low, orange glow. It made everything in her body vibrate and her breath catch in her throat. The low rumble moved through her with building excitement and she laughed out loud, reaching her hands up to the plane as if she could touch it.

"Another one's coming." He nodded toward what she knew now was a runway.

"Another?" She leapt off his lap and stood on her seat, poking her head up through the sunroof. Zach did the same, grinning over at her as the second F-16 came howling toward them. Lindsey stretched her arms to the sky as it began to take off, gaining altitude, burning fire behind. It was high above when it passed over them, and she screamed out loud in competition with the noise, her hands spread wide to the stars.

"Like it?" He smiled over at her, almost shyly.

She laughed, sliding up on the edge of the sunroof and swinging her legs over the side. "I love it! Are there more!?"

"Should be." He followed her out of the car as she went to stand in front of it, hugging her arms. "Three more."

"Hold onto me." Lindsey slipped her arms around his waist, pressing her cheek against his chest as the next one came growling toward them, the sound reverberating under her feet. His hands pressed her lower back, a little damp from dancing at the concert and now from the heat of the night, pulling her belly against his. She turned her face up to him, slipping her hand behind his neck and reaching up on tiptoe to find his mouth.

Their kiss grew hungry, and she squirmed in his arms, wanting more as the thunder of the plane grew closer, trembling her body against his. Her whole being burned, on fire, more alive than she had ever felt before. She grabbed his hand, the one pressed to her back, and urged it between her thighs, pulling it up under her skirt.

"Lindsey—" He broke their kiss, moving his hand away, but she insisted, guiding his fingers, pushing her panties aside. He groaned when he felt her smooth wetness, her lips swollen and parted in her excitement.

"Please." She gasped, her voice lost in the sound of the plane roaring overhead, but she knew he felt the urgency in her body as she pressed herself against him. The fire trailing behind the F-16 glowed for a moment like a beacon in the night, and she couldn't see anything else. His fingers moved between her legs, slowly exploring the soft folds, and he caught her mouth again, kissing her back toward the hood of the car.

"Yes, yes, yes!" She spread for him in excitement, letting him push her skirt up over her hips as she slid onto the hood of the car, pulling her own panties down. When she reached for the crotch of his jeans, aching to feel him, see him, taste him, he let her rub there for a moment. The outline of his cock straining against the denim was almost too much for her to bear, and she unsnapped his jeans, wanting to set him free.

"No."

She only heard the word he spoke because the next plane was still far off, a low rumble in the distance, a crackling fire, like the heat between her thighs. Then she couldn't hear anything but the wailing sound of the F-16 heading down the runway toward them as Zach spread her legs and sank to his knees before her.

His mouth covered her mound and he kissed her pussy like he had kissed her lips. He drank her, breathed her, and she couldn't hear the sounds he made, but they vibrated her flesh, sending delicious pulses of pleasure through her body. She threw her hands above her head, her own soft moans lost in the growing roar of the approaching plane.

When his fingers slipped into her, she bucked her hips up, meeting his hand, helping him bury first one, then two, then three into her flesh. She wanted even more and she rolled her pelvis, dancing against his mouth, her breath coming faster in the night. His tongue moved up and down in her wetness, teasing, making her arch and push against him.

His tongue finally found her clit, flicking back and forth there, and she groaned, the sound lost as the plane passed directly overhead. She watched the flaming bullet soar through the sky through half-closed eyes, the sweet ache between her thighs rising with it. Her fingers moved through his short, wiry hair, slipping her hand behind his neck and pressing him against her mound.

He opened his mouth wide over her, his tongue lapping, his fingers digging deeper. Her nails scratched over his scalp, the back of his neck, trying to press him harder, wanting more. Her body trembled on the hood of the car with her impending orgasm, and she fucked his hand faster, harder, her moans louder as she rocked against his tongue.

"Zach!" His name escaped her lips as she groped for something, anything, to hold onto. She found his other hand and squeezed it, hearing the sound of the last plane blazing toward them in the distance. "Oh god, Zach, don't stop!" He showed no signs of it, but she knew he couldn't possibly hear her anymore as the plane bellowed down the runway. She saw it mounting above her in the sky as her body sent her flying, too, twisting and shuddering with her climax.

She bucked under him, every muscle taut as she spasmed again and again under his tongue, his fingers plunging deep into her swollen flesh. Her cries, nearly screams now, were lost in the deafening boom of the plane overhead, its fire burning hot and then fading as it found its niche and rode it.

"Oh god, oh god, oh god," she whispered to the sky, blinking at the stars left in the darkness, as if the plane itself had created them in its powerful wake.

Zach pulled her to sitting, and she laughed, dizzy, resting her cheek against his chest, still panting. He held her close and she felt his heart beating hard, and smelled herself on his breath. She tilted her face up to him in the night and kissed him, tasting the sweet musk of her own pussy on his tongue, sucking at it. When her hand slipped between his legs, feeling an incredible throb there, he groaned against her mouth, stepping back with a sigh.

"I told you, baby." He leaned over to pick up her panties off the ground. "I didn't take you out to have sex with you."

"Um, what do you call that, then?" Lindsey grinned. "Bill Clinton's version? Oral sex isn't sex?"

He grinned back, handing over the sheer black material of her panties. "Well… okay, so I slipped a little."

"Let's slip some more." She wrapped her legs around his waist, tossing her panties onto the hood of the car. "Slip and slide and…"

"Nuh-uh." He pulled her off the hood of the car and she stood, wobbly, letting him hold her and pull her close. "Come on. It's almost one… and I promised your father I'd have you home."

"He's not my father." She couldn't help smiling as she pulled her panties on. He let her hold his arm for balance. "Are you for real?"

"You tell me." He went around to the passenger side of the car and opened her door, waiting. She came to stand in front of him, still feeling shaky.

"I don't know." She sighed, swallowing and looking up at him.

"You will." He smiled, tilting her chin up, and kissed her softly. "Let's get you home."

Chapter Five

"I'm afraid you can't top Kenny Wayne Shepard and an orgasm under the flight pattern of an F-16."

She loved making Zach laugh—it was deep and genuine and made her feel as warm and wiggly as a happy puppy every time she heard it. He'd called every night this week, and she couldn't seem to get enough of him, or vice versa.

"At least give me a shot at it."

"Maybe." Lindsey twisted coils around her finger. Hers was an old-style phone, the kind with a twisty white cord. She wasn't supposed to have a phone in her room at all, and had to keep coming up with new places to hide it. "What did you have in mind?"

"I'm not doing anything tonight…"

She smiled, remembering her parents' reaction when Zach dropped her off last Saturday night. "Okay."

"You're so easy."

She snorted. "You have no idea."

"Oh, I think I do."

The pause that followed hung there, and she pulled the cord tight, making the tip of her finger turn so red it was almost purple. Downstairs, she heard the side door, and knew her parents were home from shopping.

"I've gotta go."

"Tonight at seven?"

"See you then." She didn't even bother hanging up the phone—she just unplugged it from the wall and wrapped the cord around it, looking around her room for a place to hide it.

"Lindsey!" Her stepfather called from the bottom of the stairs. "Come help us carry in groceries!"

"Coming!" She shoved the phone between her mattress and the wall, putting her pillow there and pulling the covers up. He was waiting for her at the bottom of the stairs and frowned as she padded down in bare feet.

"You should put some clothes on."

"These *are* clothes." She rolled her eyes, looking down at the red bikini she put on before Zach called. Her plan was to walk down to the community pool, because it was hotter than an oven in the house, especially upstairs in her room, even with all the windows open. The air conditioning had been on the fritz for three days.

"Lindsey, I got you some Twizzlers." Her mother came in the side door, carrying two plastic grocery bags. "They were on sale."

"Cool!" She slipped by her stepfather and took the bags from her mother, going to put them on the kitchen table to sift through them. "I'm going to walk down to the pool."

"Good day for it." Her mother wiped stray hair out of her eyes and reached into one of the bags, pulling out a package of red licorice. "Why don't you just go? Your father and I can handle this."

"He's not my—"

"Lindsey." Her mother sighed, holding the package of red candy out like a peace offering. "Please. Just go."

She looked between the two of them, her stepfather now looming in the doorway. Then she shrugged. "Okay, whatever." She got a beach towel out of the linen closet and slipped on her green clogs, heading out the door. Her stepfather dug bags out of the trunk of the car and she didn't wave as she walked past.

It was a short two blocks and around a corner to their community pool, a big outdoor affair with a diving board at the deep end and a hundred kids playing in the shallow water. You were supposed to shower before going in, but no one ever did. Lindsey went through the women's dressing room, the tile floor perpetually damp, the smell of chlorine strong already. There was a small steam room near the bathroom stalls that she never saw anyone use, but she peered in as she passed just out of habit.

She'd meant to bring a book, but had left the house so quickly she forgot. She signed her name and address on the clipboard on the table and looked around for a sunny spot. Forgoing the wooden lawn chairs stacked in a corner, she spread her towel out near the fence, away from most of the moms and kids, and stretched out on her belly, opening her Twizzlers package.

Already, beads of sweat ran in little rivers down her sides and between her pale breasts. She glanced down at them and smiled. *I can definitely use the color.* That made her think of Zach—not that she wasn't already thinking about him, always thinking about him lately, in the back of her mind. Just remembering the concert, and the night they spent afterwards, when she spread herself out on the hood of his car under the stars and watched the planes take off, made her whole body feel even warmer.

She had to admit she liked Zach, and part of her really didn't want to. All sorts of bells and whistles went off in her head about him. He was dangerously safe, someone she was entirely too likely to get close to, and she didn't need that. She liked her relationships—if you wanted to call them that—loose, fast, and with no attachments. Hookups, that's what they were. She hadn't ever really "dated" anyone before like she suddenly found herself doing with Zach. She didn't know if she liked it.

Rolling over onto her back, she sucked on the end of her red licorice, closing her eyes against the brightness of the sun. No matter what she did, she could still feel Zach's hands pressing her thighs open and the delicious attention of his tongue. She also remembered the way he held her, and told her he wouldn't let anything hurt her. That made her feel warm in a different place.

"Hey there, sexy girl."

Lindsey shaded her eyes, blinking up at the figure dripping over her. The cool droplets of water felt good on her skin, but she didn't recognize him at first. When he sat beside her on the cement, he shook his head like a dog and sprayed water over her belly and legs.

"Hey!" She half sat, meeting his eyes, and then she remembered—Ralph, the dark-haired senior from Xavier from the tree fort that day. She recalled the way they had taken her, forced her, made her do things, and her body burned with the memory.

"It's hotter than fuck out here." His eyes moved over her body, down over the tiny triangles of her bikini top, over her smooth, taut belly, to the red material that disappeared between her legs. He lowered his voice along with his eyes. "Well... maybe not hotter than fucking *you*."

Lindsey grinned. "Aww, you know all the right things to say to a girl, don'tcha?"

"I try."

She eyed him, licking the end of her Twizzler, back and forth with her tongue. "Been here long?"

"I dunno." He shrugged, hugging his knees and looking over at her. "Hour or so I guess." His eyes kept falling to the slope of her thighs and the bright red shock of cloth between them. Lindsey shifted on the towel, spreading her legs slightly.

"Water warm?"

"Colder than a whore's heart." He gave her a wink and then grinned. "Wanna go in?"

"Not if it's that cold!" Lindsey put a knee up and let it fall to the side, drawing his eyes again. "Maybe I'll lie in the sun for a while and then just go home."

"Aw, don't go." He turned toward her, sitting cross-legged, his knees touching her thigh. "You're the first interesting thing that's happened here today."

"What's so interesting about me?" She took a bite of her licorice, chewing thoughtfully.

"I can think of one thing right off the top of my head."

She raised her eyebrows. "Just one?"

"Okay." He grinned back, his eyes dark as they moved over her body. "A few."

She moved the red end of the licorice back and forth over her lower lip, watching his eyes follow it like a dog watching each bite of his master's dinner. Experimenting, she trailed the wet end of the licorice over her bikini top, tracing circles down her belly and around her navel. His gaze followed it.

"Do I make your cock hard?" She bit her lip, slapping the licorice strand lower across her belly.

His eyes moved between her legs. "As a fucking rock."

"Good." She rolled to her belly, pushing herself up into an arch and stretching before gathering her towel and moving to stand. "Wanna meet me in the little girls' room?"

"Yeah." He licked his lips, and the lust in his eyes made her pussy ache. She remembered his cock—how big and hard—the way he grabbed her when he fucked her. His eyes followed her as she walked away. She could feel them, and put a little extra swing into her slim hips.

When she stopped at the edge of the pool, she glanced over her shoulder and winked, dropping her towel and licorice and diving into the deep end. The water was an incredibly cold shock to her system, making her shudder as she came back up, reaching for the ladder. Water fell off her in sheets as she pulled herself up, adjusting her bikini straps when she reached the top of the ladder.

"You were right." She reached for her towel, giving him a small half-smile. "Colder than a whore's heart." He grinned, his eyes bright as he watched her dripping body stretching in the sun. She leaned in toward him, rubbing her hair with the towel, and whispered, "But her tight little cunt's still nice and hot."

"Don't I know it." He adjusted himself in his swim trunks.

"Don't be long." Lindsey grabbed her licorice and slung the towel over her shoulder, padding toward the ramp that led down to the bathrooms. Her body tingled in anticipation, and she sat on one of the benches in the women's room, waiting. The door was propped open and she sat in line of sight of it. She sighed when a woman and her two kids came down the ramp, turning into the women's room.

"But I don't *want* to go home!" The little girl pulled on her mother's arm, whining. The boy was pouting, too, but not being vocal.

"We'll stop and get McDonalds." The mother gave Lindsey a weary smile. *Way to bribe them, Mom!* It worked, though, and the kids perked up. The mother's eyes lingered over Lindsey's bikini, and she wondered if the woman even knew she was doing it. Lindsey saw Ralph glance in and gave him a little shake of her head. She was afraid the kids were going to say they had to go to the bathroom or something, but the mom pulled them along, giving her another tired smile, before going out the exit.

When Ralph passed by again, she crooked her finger at him and he slipped in, glancing around surreptitiously. "Are we alone?"

"For now." Lindsey stood, leaving her towel and candy on the bench. "Come on."

He followed her around the corner, into the cubicle past the women's bathroom stalls. She pulled open the door to the steam room and gasped at the heat.

"In there?"

She shrugged, slipping through the door and motioning for him to follow. "No one ever uses it."

"Fuck!" He gasped, too, waving uselessly at the steam rising around them. "It's hot in here."

"I think that's the idea." Lindsey reached behind her neck, untying the red strings of her bikini top and letting them fall. "But I think it might get hotter."

He watched as she reached behind her to unhook her suit in back, letting it drop. He eyed her breasts as she tweaked her nipples, making them stand up. "I'll say."

Her whole body felt wet and sticky with steam. She tugged at her bikini bottoms, but they stuck at her hips and began to roll down. Ralph's hand moved under his own suit as he watched her struggle with the material. Finally she got them down, kicking them aside and putting one foot up on one of the slatted wooden benches.

"God, you've got a nice pussy." Ralph watched as she slid her fingers down to show him her pink, and he moved closer to get a better view in the rising steam.

"You like it?" She slipped up onto the bench, putting her other foot up and spreading her legs wide. Her fingers moved up and down her slit, teasing her aching clit. His hand moved faster under his trunks and she wanted to see his cock. "Do you want it?"

"You have no idea."

"Oh, I think I do." She slid a finger inside, then two, fucking herself slowly. "Show me that hard cock." He didn't hesitate, sliding his swim trucks off and letting his dick spring free. It rose high out of a dark thatch of hair, throbbing in his hand. It made her mouth water just looking at it.

"Will you suck it?" He moved close enough so she could see the veins pulsing along the underside as he stroked it.

Her narrowed eyes moved up to meet his and she frowned. "Don't ask me."

He looked confused for a moment, cocking his head at her, and then a light came into his eyes. A slow smile spread over his face and she gasped when his hand gripped her hair, pulling her head back.

"Suck my fucking cock." He shoved it between her lips and she moaned, her fingers moving faster in her pussy as he began to fuck her mouth. His fist tightened in her hair when she struggled against him, trying desperately to catch her breath in the steam heat. It was like trying to breathe through a wet washcloth, and his cock throbbed as he slid it deep into the back of her throat. "God, you're a hungry little cock whore, aren't you?"

Lindsey's pussy ached for something more but she swallowed around his cock, using her tongue to lick the head before he shoved it back into her throat again. He used her mouth just like a cunt, groaning loudly as he fucked her face, harder and deeper, his breath coming faster. She whimpered around his shaft, her sopping fingers buried deep inside her pussy, her thumb strumming at her clit.

When he pulled her off his cock, there was an audible sound of the suction breaking, a fat "pop," and she looked up at him with bleary eyes, her mouth swollen and red. He slapped at her cheeks with it, teasing her tongue, and she licked at it and tried to suck it back in, but he wouldn't let her. His fist in her hair pulled her mouth back, making her gasp out loud.

"I'm gonna fuck that tight little pussy."

She slid her fingers out, lifting them to her mouth and sucking them. "Oh Brer Bear, don't throw me in the briar patch!" His grip tightened as he pulled her to standing, mashing his mouth against hers, sucking at her tongue. She grabbed his cock, pumping it in her fist, rubbing it over the wet heat of her belly and edging it down between her swollen lips. It was the wrong angle, but she rubbed it there anyway, teasing her clit with his cock as they kissed and panted together in the heat.

"Turn around." He shoved her about, grabbing her slim hips and pulling them into his. His cock rose like an iron bar between her thighs and she squeezed them around his shaft, feeling it throb. The vapor, which had begun to dissipate slightly, began to rise around them again as the steam kicked back on. The heat was incredible and Lindsey thought she would pass out as his fingers probed between her lips in search of her hole.

She moaned when he found it, arching back. He kept his fingers there as a guide, using his other hand to ease the head of his cock along her slick slit, positioning himself. Her hands gripped the wooden slats, and she bit her lip, her whole body trembling in anticipation of that first deep, hard thrust.

She wasn't disappointed. Ralph gave a low grunt, gripping her hips and shoving in so hard she had to put her hands up to the wall to keep from falling forward. His cock was deliciously big, spreading her wide as he began to fuck her. Lindsey caught his rhythm, closing her eyes and leaning into the wall, resting her cheek there. The tiled surface was cooler than the air around them, and she moaned against it, meeting his thrusts with her own.

"Harder!" she gasped, going up on her tiptoes, looking for a deeper angle. He groaned, reaching forward to grasp one of her breasts, squeezing her nipple and then twisting it hard. That made her squeal, the sensation sending a hot fire of pain that turned to pleasure in an instant spreading down toward her pussy.

"Goddamnit, I said harder!" Lindsey reached between her legs, finding his balls and rubbing them against her clit. He gasped, grabbing her hair and shoving her sideways onto the bench, using all of his weight to press her down. She couldn't breathe and she didn't want to as he laid her out, driving his cock into her from behind. He was fully on her now and using all of his strength to fuck her wide open.

"Oh fuck!" He groaned, slowing a little, and she knew he was close. Her whole pussy felt swollen and slick with the fuck, and she reached behind her to feel him as he knelt up between her thighs, digging for a deeper angle. His hands grabbed her hips and he found it, shoving into her hard.

"Come on!" Lindsey taunted, reaching back and spreading her ass with both hands as he fucked her, lifting her hips. "If you really want that cunt, then *use* it!" He grabbed her wrists, both of them, pulling her back as he pressed forward into her, his cock twitching fast. He was really close.

"Come all over my slutty little cunt!" She moaned the words, rocking her hips, squeezing her pussy hard around his shaft. "Do it! Now!"

He did as she asked, pulling out of her with a low groan and flooding her pussy with his cum. She felt a thick spurt of it land across her thigh like a brand, and the next fat shot swelled over her lips, easing down her slit in a hot gush. She felt him shuddering behind her as he pumped his cock in his fist, rubbing the head of it over her flesh as he came.

Lindsey wiggled away, rolling over onto her back, and threw an arm over her eyes. Her panting breath began to slow just a little, but she still felt like she was going to pass out, between the level of her arousal and the incredible heat of the steam room. She heard the door open and didn't look up. He was going, and that was just fine.

Her fingers moved between her legs, finding the sticky wet heat of his cum, and rubbing it in. Alone now, her memory returned to the moment, the grab and push and pull of it, the resistance and the taking. Her pussy burned, and her sticky fingers moved faster over her clit, her lungs pulling in thick steam in huge, gasping gulps.

"Oh god!" she whispered, circling her clit. "Please, oh god." And she found that it wasn't Ralph fucking her, using her, that pushed her over. It was the image of Zach, his face buried between her legs, and the deafening sound of the planes above their heads. It was Zach's hands, his tongue, his eyes, and she was coming in his mouth, her hips bucking up to meet him as he held her in his grip.

She heard herself call his name and opened her eyes in surprise in the white mist, her body still shivering from her climax. She was, indeed, alone. Glancing down at her discarded red suit on the floor, she felt something turn over in her belly. Zach was coming to pick her up tonight.

Standing, she felt Ralph's cum sliding down her thigh, and grimaced. When she opened the door to the steam room, she gratefully gulped the cool air and headed naked for a shower stall with her suit balled up in her fist. She had never felt a greater need in her life to get clean than she did in that moment.

Chapter Six

"Lindsey Renee Anderson!"

She knew she was in trouble when her mother used her full name. The pounding on the bathroom door just wouldn't stop. *I don't have time for this.* Zach was due to pick her up any minute.

"What?" She opened her eyes wide as she leaned over the sink, applying mascara, her mouth a perfectly round "O."

"Your father and I need to talk to you."

She stopped mid-stroke with her mascara brush, her eyes narrowing, and she gave an evil look toward the door. Her mouth formed the words, but no sound came out: *"He's not my father!"* There was the pounding again, and this time her stepfather's voice.

"Lindsey! If you intend to leave this house at all tonight, I suggest you come out and talk to us!"

I'll leave if I want to, asshole. She shoved the mascara brush violently back into the container, screwing on the lid and throwing it into her make-up bag. She adjusted the long peasant skirt she was wearing, glancing in the mirror to make sure the white satin shorts she wore underneath didn't show.

"I'm coming!" She made a kissing face at her own reflection, tilting her head first left, then right. The pink tank-tee she was wearing wasn't made to be see-through, but without a bra, her dark nipples were clearly visible. Grabbing her purse and slinging it over her shoulder, she pulled the door open and crossed her arms in front of her chest. "Jeez! Can't a girl even take a pee without it turning into some committee meeting?"

They all stood there, arms crossed, glaring for a moment, before Lindsey's mother broke the silence. "You look nice."

"Thanks." Lindsey snapped her gum. "So what's up? Zach'll be here any minute." Her parents exchanged looks and she knew, then, what they were up to and rolled her eyes. "Oh good god, don't tell me this is the 'you can't date a nee-gro' lecture again?'" She brushed past them both and headed toward the kitchen.

"It's not that." Her mother's voice followed her, and so did her stepfather's footsteps. The whole kitchen still smelled like stuffed green peppers, which Lindsey hadn't touched. She hated green stuff. "It's just... well, Zach is a little old for you, don't you think?"

Lindsey snagged a Diet Coke, popping the lid open with a pink-painted fingernail. "Twenty-two is too old?" She downed half the can in four big swallows and then burped loudly. "Christ, it could be so much worse. He could be fifty-two—lay off already!"

Her mother sat at the kitchen table and sighed, glancing up at her stepfather. He just shrugged, shaking his head. Lindsey hid a smile behind her Coke can, swallowing the rest of it. It thrilled her to know that she had backed them into a corner. They were too P.C. to say any more about the fact that he was black, and they couldn't really soundly object to their four-year age difference.

"Four years isn't a big deal if you're, say, thirty, and he's thirty-four..." Her stepfather was clearly trying to salvage his argument. "But there's a big difference when you're eighteen and he's twenty-two."

"Really?" Lindsey rolled her eyes, tossing the can into the recycling bin. "Is that the new math? Did I miss that day in school?"

"Honey…" Her mother sighed again, folding her hands on the marred surface of the table. It was the one piece of furniture they'd had since she was a baby, and she suddenly had a memory of her father—her real father—sitting her on the edge of that table, putting a band-aid on her knee after she'd fallen down and skinned it. *That can't be a real memory. I was too young. I must have seen a picture of it or something…* But she knew it was. She had only a few memories of him at all, but that was one.

"Wait!" Lindsey held up her hand. She'd heard Zach's Camaro pull up in the driveway. "Let me save you some breath. You're worried about me… *concerned about my welfare,* that's all. You wouldn't even be having this conversation with me if you didn't love me so much. Right?"

"I don't appreciate your sarcasm." Her stepfather's jaw was working in that way it did before he really got mad, and she was glad she was minutes from heading out the door.

"And I don't appreciate you trying to tell me who I can or can't see." Lindsey heard Zach's footsteps on the stairs. "I'm not going to tell this guy to come back in the year 2020 because you're afraid of the age difference. That's just wack!"

The doorbell rang. That was her cue. "So tell me, mom… which do you hate most? The fact that he's black? Or the fact that he's twenty-two?"

"Which attracts you most?" her stepfather asked, leaning against the doorframe, his arms crossed.

Her mother shook her head, waving her hand in dismissal. "It doesn't matter. Just go, Lindsey. You're going to do whatever you want to do. You always have, and you always will."

"You got that one right." She edged by her stepfather, heading for the front door and the promise of another night with Zach.

"Lindsey!" Her stepfather's voice was a warning, but she didn't stop. When she opened the door, there was Zach, waiting in the dusky light, whistling some tune. He smiled when he saw her, glancing down at her long, flowing skirt, his eyes widening in surprise.

"You look nice."

She snorted, taking his hand and pulling him down the porch steps. "I'm changing in the car."

He laughed, shaking his head as he opened the passenger door for her. "Don't tell me—you're wearing the 'come-fuck-me-shorts' under there?"

"How did you guess?" She was already wiggling the elastic waist of the skirt down over her hips when he slid in, putting the key into the ignition. "Thought I'd give you a great big hint."

"Damn, girl." Zach glanced over as she slid the skirt down her slim thighs, kicking it into a ball on the floor next to her sandals and putting her now-bare feet up on the dash. Her toes were painted pink. "You sure do make it hard to say no."

"I hope so." She grinned over at him, pushing the button to roll down the window and putting her face up to the breeze. "So where are we going tonight?"

"It's not far." He smiled over at her as she turned up the radio, leaning her seat back a little and dangling her arm out the window. Her hand danced in the breeze.

"You're big on surprises, aren't you?" The air was warm, even though it was near dark already and she twisted to put her feet out the window, too.

"Do you want me to tell you?"

She contemplated this, chewing her gum. "No."

"I think you like surprises." Zach steered the car around a corner.

"Good ones, sure." Lindsey gave a half-snort, half-laugh. "It's the bad ones that get me."

"Like what?" It sounded like a casual question, but she knew better. She could feel herself closing, something in her snapping tight. Telling people about what went on inside Lindsey wasn't ever part of the deal. The good thing was, it was pretty easy to get most guys to talk about themselves.

"Oh, you know, the usual stuff." She flipped the radio station. "So have you been overseas yet in this war thing?"

Zach was quiet and for a moment she thought her tactic hadn't worked. "I've been on two tours in Iraq, yes."

"How was it?"

"Lonely." He shrugged, and she saw his eyes moving over her thighs. She slid down a little further in her seat. "I spent six months in a submarine, five hundred meters under the surface of the Indian Ocean."

"Six months?" She stared at him, incredulous.

"Actually, eight months on the second tour."

"But you never saw any action?" She snapped her gum, changing the station again.

Zach reached over and turned off the radio. "I'll talk about it if you really want me to, but don't use it to just try and change the subject, okay?"

She flushed, glad for the coming darkness. The next words that came out of her mouth surprised them both. "My father was killed in Iraq."

"I'm sorry, Lindsey."

"I was very little." She shrugged, shocked at herself. There wasn't one other person in the world she could remember ever speaking those words out loud to. "I don't remember much about him."

"It was Desert Storm?"

She nodded, pulling her feet into the car and sitting up. "He was in the army. I guess he got lured in by that whole college education and a free ride spiel." Zach didn't say anything, he just drove, but she knew he was listening. "You know, that whole travel to exotic, foreign lands, meet new and interesting people…and kill them?"

"I'm familiar with the concept."

"Except he was the one who got killed."

Zach shook his head. "There were only about two hundred total U.S. casualties in Desert Storm."

"Yeah." She gave him a wry smile. "Talk about bad surprises. But that's my luck for you…I inherited it from my mother."

"So it's been just you and your mom since?"

"My stepdad came into the picture when I was about five or six."

"You don't like him very much."

She turned her face out toward the window. "So, you never said, did you see any action?"

"I was on a fast-attack sub. We had a few hunter-killer missions. That's what we were there to do." He glanced over and she felt his eyes on her. "I take it you don't like talking about your stepfather?"

"Hey, look at that, we're here." She leaned forward as he pulled into a parking lot. "Where's here?"

"Okay, I can take a hint." Zach opened his door.

She rolled her eyes as she got out, turning her bottom toward him and rubbing the satin seat of her shorts. "Promises, promises."

"Come on, sexy." He smacked her behind on the way past, popping the trunk. "Let's see if I can top front row seats at Kenny Wayne Shepard followed by an orgasm under the flight pattern of an F-16."

She raised her eyebrows as he took a guitar case out. "Why…are you planning two orgasms?"

"Could be." He grinned, slipping his arm around her waist as he led her toward a darkly lit building. She heard music already, a low, steady beat.

She showed her fake I.D. at the door and they went into a little blues bar, smoky and dark inside and packed with people. Zach ordered himself a beer and Lindsey a Coke and she rolled her eyes at that, but drank it thirstily as they searched for a seat near the front of the stage. The band was playing a cover of Stevie Ray Vaughan's Double Trouble and Zach left his guitar on the edge of the stage, giving a nod to the lead singer.

They gave up on looking for a place to sit and Lindsey wrinkled her nose at Zach as she led him out onto the dance floor, but it was too loud for her to ask what was up. Besides, the music made her want to take her clothes off, and if she couldn't do that, at the very least, she wanted to be pressed between the sea of bodies, as close to Zach as she could get.

She got her wish. The dance floor was almost as packed as the tables had been. Wrapping her arms up around Zach's neck, she rubbed the front of her body against him, shifting her hips into his. His eyes lit up as he watched her, his hands resting at her waist, and she smiled as their bodies moving in easy synch. Most guys she dated did the usual white-boy snap and sway, but her body knew immediately that Zach could really *dance.*

When the song ended, he dragged her, protesting, off the floor. She flagged a waitress while he was up at the front of the stage, talking to the lead singer during a lull in their set, and ordered three shots of whiskey. Zach turned just as she was about to down the last one, and snatched it from her, making a face.

"Hey!" she protested, grabbing for it.

"No way." He tossed it back himself, grimacing. "If you want, I'll get you a beer."

She rolled her eyes and crossed her arms but accepted the beer when the waitress came over with it. Lindsey saw the way the woman looked at Zach, the way she rubbed her ample chest "accidentally" against his arm when she set the beer on the table they'd managed to squeeze in at. The waitress shot her a dirty look when she turned to go, and Lindsey made a face at her back, knowing immediately it was a racial thing.

"Where are you going?" Lindsey grasped Zach's arm as he headed toward the stage.

He grinned and shook her off. "You'll see."

Of course, the guitar case should have tipped her off. She actually thought he might just know the lead singer or something and was dropping it off for him. It hadn't occurred to her that he was going to play—or sing. He strapped the guitar on, giving her a wink as the band started playing behind him. He'd clearly planned this, and she smiled, tipping her beer at him before taking a long swig.

It was after the first stanza of the song, well into the verse, that Lindsey realized he was singing to her—*about* her. She looked up at him with wide eyes for a moment, blinking fast. She recognized the song well enough—it was the Fabulous Thunderbirds.

"You're hot, too hot, too hot to handle…
Let me tell you people
I'm only a man
I didn't realize
what I held in my hands…"

She grinned up at him then, shaking her head, and he winked again, his eyes meeting hers over the microphone. His fingers were long and deft, working the guitar strings effortlessly, and Lindsey watched, a slow burn heating her belly. She'd been attracted to him from the moment she met him, but seeing him up on stage, hearing the low, rough edge to his voice, she wanted nothing more than to find somewhere to get naked with him—fast.

"When she enters the room
Men hide their wedding rings
I know what you're thinking
You're thinkin' about that wild thing.
I know she's hot, too hot, too hot to handle…"

The music was too hot not to move, and she danced near the front of the stage, her eyes on his. He watched her grind her hips around and around, her arms above her head, her belly undulating with the beat. When the song was over, he thanked the band, and hopped off the stage to join her. She opened her mouth to say something when the waitress sidled in between them, smiling up at Zach.

"You were hot, honey!" The woman's nails were as long as claws and she trailed one of them down the front of Zach's shirt like an orange streak, hooking her finger in his belt and tugging slightly. "You can play for me anytime!"

"You itchin' to leave here on a stretcher?" Lindsey stepped in next to Zach, snatching the woman's hand away from his belt buckle.

"Go away, little girl." The woman rolled her eyes, waving Lindsey away and turning back to Zach.

He opened his mouth to say something, but Lindsey stepped in, grabbing the woman's white, low-cut blouse in her fist. "I'll kick your ass so hard you'll have to rent stilts to wipe yourself."

The woman's eyes showed fear for a moment and she shook loose, taking a step back and glaring at her. "Are you even legal?"

Zach turned back to grab his guitar case off the stage. "Come on, baby." He steered Lindsey past the waitress by the elbow. She stopped to grab her beer on the way as he guided her through the crowd. When they got into the parking lot, she glanced up at him and saw he was tight-lipped.

"What did I do?" She frowned as he put the guitar case in the trunk and opened her door for her. "I wasn't the one being Ms. Uber-Slut…for once!"

He sighed, his face softening. "Just get in."

She did, pouting, putting her beer in the beverage holder and obediently pulling her seatbelt on. Glancing over at him as he started the car, she sighed. "I'm sorry."

He shook his head and gave her a small smile. "Never mind. Let's go get a burger or something."

Heartened, she turned towards him, her knee knocking the beer in the holder. It tilted onto the floor and she gasped. "Oh shit!" Her skirt was soaked, and she grabbed the foaming bottle, putting it back into the holder and sopping the floor up the best she could with the material. "I'm sorry!"

"Two sorries in one night." Zach laughed. "Is that a record for you?"

She stuck her tongue out at him, hurt, and held up her skirt. "Damn. I can't go home in this. Even if it dries, it smells like a distillery."

"Maybe it's a sign." He smiled as he put the car in gear and she smiled back when he reached over and squeezed her hand.

* * * *

"I think you should throw these in." Lindsey snapped the elastic on her white satin shorts with a grin, watching Zach throw her skirt into his stacked apartment washing machine.

"Did you get those, too?" He glanced over at her as she slid up onto the bathroom sink, pulling her knee up and resting her chin there.

"Sort of." Her eyes followed him as he poured in soap and set the timer. "After listening to you tonight, I'd say I need to change my panties…if I was wearing any." She saw his eyes dip between her thighs and smiled. "So…now what?"

He came to stand between her thighs, slipping his arms around her waist. "So you liked tonight?"

"Yeah." She slid her arms around his neck, wiggling against him as she wrapped her legs around his waist. "I did. A lot."

He kissed the top of her head and she felt him breathe deep. "It was hard to beat the other night."

"Oh, I don't know." Her fingers worked the buttons on his shirt from top to bottom, and he let her. "I think we can still make it."

"No F-16's." His hands cupped her behind, pulling her in tighter to him. She felt the heat of his cock, already half-hard, and squirmed against it.

"I don't think we need 'em." She lifted her face to his to be kissed and wasn't disappointed. The energy of the night caught between them spread through her as their mouths and bodies met. Her fingers traced his chest and belly, thrilling at the hard ridges and smooth planes as his big hands clenched her behind, pulling her snugly into the saddle of his hips.

The heat and hardness of him teased her, and the already damp crotch of her shorts slipped between her lips as they rocked. She moaned into his mouth, sucking at his tongue and digging her heels into his lower back. Twice she reached for his zipper and he caught her hand, moving it to more neutral territory, all the while exploring her mouth with his.

The ache in her belly slowly turned to fire and she squeezed her legs around him, dancing her hips against his cock just like she had gyrated for him on the dance floor. That made him groan and grip her hair as he slanted his mouth across hers. His response was encouraging and she reached for him again. This time he didn't say no, and her hand rubbed the length of him through the thick denim, slowly up and down.

"Oh damn." His words were just breath in her ear and she heard him swallow. "Lindsey…"

"Just my mouth." She panted with him, and didn't even recognize the plea in her voice. "Let me suck you…oh god, please."

"Just…" Her kiss stopped him and she found his tongue, using hers to tease it, sucking at it like a little cock, making his hips buck into hers. She smiled through their kiss as he lifted her and carried her like that, wrapped around him, out of the bathroom. The layout of his place wasn't familiar enough to her, but she knew when he turned right instead of left, pushing through a door, that they were going into the bedroom. It smelled like Zach in here, cool and clean.

There were no words as he kissed her against the wall, not even making it all the way over to the bed in his lust, pressing his full weight onto her. She took it, greedy, grateful, tugging his shirt off his shoulders. The material stuck at the sleeves, where it was buttoned, and he sighed at the annoyance as he let her down and undid them. She pressed the seam of her shorts against her clit as she watched him, rubbing it back and forth there with her fingers. His eyes met hers as he tossed his shirt aside and bent to kiss her again.

Welcoming the weight of him, she pushed her pelvis up, angling, seeking his hard length and finding it with the rock of her hips. He nuzzled his way down her neck, pulling her pink tank-tee up over her little breasts and capturing one of her nipples in his mouth. She sighed happily as his tongue made soft circles there, his fingers finding and squeezing the other one, making it stand up.

Replacing his tongue with his other hand, he rolled both of her nipples as he kissed his way down her bare belly. Lindsey wiggled when he dipped his tongue into her navel, knowing just what he was up to, and she wasn't having any of it.

"No, you don't." She squirmed out from under his weight, turning so she pressed him against the wall. His hands and eyes roamed over her, his fingers moving her shorts aside and she saw his eyes darken at the sight of her shaved pussy. "I told you what I wanted."

"Do you always get what you want?" Zach let her go and she slithered between his legs, unbuttoning his jeans and working his zipper down. She didn't answer him—she was too engrossed in freeing his cock. It was just as beautiful—and big—as it had felt through the denim. Tugging his pants down his hips, she was gratified when he helped her get them and his boxers to his knees, his cock springing free and pointing straight up toward the ceiling.

"More than a mouthful." Lindsey swallowed, grasping his shaft in her hand and noticing how slender and pale her fingers seemed in comparison to the thick, dark length of him. He was beautifully uncircumcised, the head already leaking a clearish fluid. She rubbed it over her lips like gloss, looking up at him. "Tell me what you want."

"I want to eat that sweet, bald little pussy of yours, girl." His thumb moved over her bottom lip, rubbing his pre-cum in there. "Come up here."

"But don't you want my mouth?" She teased the frenulum, following the sweet groove with the tip of her tongue. "I've been told I'm pretty good at giving head."

He chuckled. "I bet you have. Now get your hot little ass up here."

"Nuh-uh." She took him in her mouth, using her best deep-throating technique to work him back into her throat. It wasn't easy and she fought her gag-reflex, forcing even more of him in. He groaned, his eyes wide as he watched her pink lips grow taut, enveloping his dark length. Still, she couldn't make it all the way down on him and she came up for air with a gasp, leaving a slick trail of saliva in her wake.

Her hand didn't stop, though, and she used it to stroke him from base to tip, easing the loose skin up over the head and down again as she looked at his cock, renegotiating just exactly how she was going to take him.

"I said..." He reached down and grabbed her by the back of her shorts, hauling her around. She gasped, hearing the small sound of the fabric tearing a little, probably somewhere along the seam, and she squealed as he situated her hips over his face. "Come here."

"Zach!" Her hand never left his cock as he lifted her. It just twisted around the shaft as he turned her, and she squeezed him hard when his fingers shoved her shorts aside and probed between her lips. He used one hand to spread her open, his fingers tracing her pink folds of flesh, while he kept his other arm wrapped tight around her hips to keep her steady. It was a great distraction and she found it more and more difficult to concentrate on the cock she had taken again into her mouth.

He carried her that way toward the bed, her lips and tongue working his cock, his face buried in the soft wetness of her pussy. He hummed gently over her clit as she sucked him, wrapping both arms around her hips and ass and pulling her up snug against his mouth. All the blood rushed to Lindsey's head and she flushed with it, hanging onto his cock, dizzy and upside down.

When he eased her down onto the bed, he rolled so she was on top of him and she gasped as his fingers, now free to roam, pressed between her lips, probing her flesh. His tongue moved, relentless, varying both speed and direction, leaving her breathless and guessing what he was going to do next. She couldn't even keep a steady rhythm on his cock anymore, so she rested her cheek against his thigh and just stroked up and down his length.

"Oh god, baby…" she whispered, rocking her hips as he fingered her, two and then three, spreading her wide as he tongued her slit. "You make my pussy feel so good!"

He groaned against her clit, licking faster, making his tongue flat and edging it wetly back and forth until she thought she would go crazy with wanting him. Her whole body felt as if it were on fire, and his cock throbbed in her hand, forgotten entirely, a steady pulse in her fist.

"Ohhhhh fuck!" Lindsey felt it coming and worked for it, her hips rolling in circles, her teeth raking along his thigh. She let go of his cock, propping herself up with her palms on his thighs and grinding her pussy down against his face. He took her with a muffled groan, wrapping his arms around her ass and burying his face into her wetness.

Her nails dug into the hard muscles of his thighs as she came, shuddering and throwing her head back, bucking on top of him, completely oblivious to anything but the flood of throbbing heat between her legs that went on and on. He sucked hard at her sensitive clit, making her thrash and squeal and beg him to stop, the pleasure so intense it made her grit her teeth.

"Please!" she begged, unable to wiggle her way out of his hard grasp.

"You wanted to suck my cock, didn't you?" He came up for air, gasping, giving her a brief respite. "So suck it, baby!"

She groaned, remembering him then, spitting on her hand and slicking her fist down over the head of him like a wet little pussy and following it with the softness of her lips and mouth and tongue, making him press deeper. Her hand prevented too much of him from sliding into her throat, but even that wasn't enough to keep her from gagging entirely on his thick length.

His rubbed his face into her wetness again, making her moan and shift on top of him, not sure if she wanted to try to get away or press back against his tongue. It was his finger that decided her, the one that slid out of her pussy to stroke the tender ring of her asshole. He kept two working and buried in her pussy, but his index finger found its way to the sweet pucker of her ass, making wet circles there as he tongued her clit into submission again.

This time she was determined not to lose her focus, and she worked his cock for everything she was worth, forcing more and more of it into her throat with every pass. Her hand grew slick with her saliva mixed with a steady flow of his pre-cum, more copious and thick as she sucked harder and harder. When she pulled the skin of his cock down tight and used her tongue under the uncircumcised edge, seeking out the sensitive ridge, he groaned and bucked up, making her gasp when his finger slipped deeper into her ass.

"Oh yeah!" He managed a muffled groan as she stayed tucked under the skin there and stroked him against the curve of her tongue. She eased the skin up and down, squeezing her fist as she went, faster and faster. Her tongue curved around his shaft, making a little cup, and she waited for him to fill it. "Oh god! Baby!"

She knew the warning tone and pumped faster, her other hand slipping down to feel how close to his body his balls had drawn, the skin tight and wrinkled and deliciously smooth under her fingers. She cupped them, imagining all of the cum in there, waiting to burst and flood into her mouth. The thought made her dizzy with wanting it, and she couldn't hold out anymore against his fingers and tongue.

Her whole body shuddered against his, but she didn't stop working his cock. She felt the muscles in his belly growing tighter against her breasts, their skin slick, bodies rocking hard and fast. Suddenly his cock swelled in her hand, and the first blast of his cum wasn't just a flood over her tongue—it shot hard and fast and thick, coating the back of her throat and forcing her to swallow immediately. He shoved up into her mouth, thrust himself deeper into her throat, and it was he who forgot about her this time, moaning against her pussy, his tongue and lips losing all focus and direction.

She shivered happily on top of him, still grinding her own orgasm against his chin and nose and mouth as she milked his throbbing cock. The second and third waves of his cum weren't as strong as the first, but they filled her mouth both times to almost bursting. She swallowed fast before taking the next, and then another, the taste coating her tongue and throat as she eagerly pumped his length.

When she climbed off him and turned around to steal a kiss, he pulled her in tight. She shivered when his tongue met hers and he grabbed for the comforter, fisting it and pulling it over them, wrapping her in it. Smiling, she tucked her head under his chin, feeling her eyes slipping closed before she even knew what was happening. Never had she felt more comfortable and safe with a man. It would be hours before either of them remembered time, or space, or anything but drifting away in each other's arms on a cloud far away in the darkness.

Chapter Seven

"Run down that aisle and grab me some laundry detergent, would you?"

"Fine." Lindsey sighed, hugging herself and shivering as she followed her mother pushing the cart past the meat bins. *Should have worn jeans or something.* She smiled to herself at the thought of actually complying with her mother's wishes and wearing more clothes than she had on. They'd compromised on a pair of Daisy Duke cutoffs and a tube top. She still couldn't wear her white satin short shorts out of the house without protest. "Are we almost done?"

"Just a few more things on my list." Her mother peered at something written on the back of a receipt as Lindsey headed toward the soap aisle. "You know what brand to get, right?"

"Not exactly the first time you've sent me looking for detergent."

Her mother sighed. "Hurry back, I'll be over by the baked goods."

"Ooo, get some donuts!" Lindsey's eyes brightened at the thought.

"Breakfast of champions?" Her mother snorted.

"Breakfast of teenagers. Please?"

Her mother sighed again. "Hurry back and you can pick some out."

Lindsey hefted an orange bottle of Tide from the bottom shelf. It made her think of Zach and the way he had tossed her clothes in his little stackable washer and dryer in his apartment. That hadn't been the last time she'd seen him—they'd had two more dates with just a kiss at her doorstep, which had left her both confused and annoyed. And then there was the couch incident.

She balanced the detergent against her hip, remembering the last time she was by his place. She'd thought it might have happened then, when they were together on the couch. Zach must have thought they'd be safer in the living room than the bedroom, but Lindsey could maneuver her little body into all sorts of positions, and had managed to free his cock, pulling her shorts and panties aside so she was rubbing up against him as they kissed.

The feel of her hot, slick cunt riding up and down his shaft should have done it—that and, of course, all the begging and pleading and dirty talk she was doing in his ear. It was certainly having an effect on his cock. It was rock hard and weeping, his hands digging deep into the flesh of her hips and ass as she rubbed against him, and his groans were definitely caught somewhere between pleasure and pain.

"Please, baby, please," she begged him, her tank-tee pulled up over her little breasts, the nipples hard as she rocked faster. "God, I can't stand it, Zach, I want you, I want your cock in me, baby, ohhh god please fuck me, please, please…" She wasn't even sure of the words, she was just begging him, aching for him—she honestly couldn't remember a time when she had wanted sex so much, not for real. He made her head swim.

"Lindsey, listen…" He always tried talking, some rational discussion, some logical reason why not, but she didn't want to hear it and would do anything *not* to hear it.

"Suck my tits," she moaned, directing her nipple into his mouth. "Please, god, suck it hard. Sometimes I can come that way."

That made him groan and draw her nipple into his mouth with a ferocious hunger, working the other one between his big fingers. She thrashed and twisted in his lap, working her hips in fast, hot circles over his dick, sure that if she came this way, if he reduced her to a wet, quivering puddle of cum on his couch, he would have to fuck her—he wouldn't be able to stop himself.

"Baby, god, that's it!" she cried, thrusting her hips against his, feeling her climax coming. He mouthed her other nipple, sucking it hard and sending her right over the edge. Lindsey quivered on his lap, her pussy clamping down against his cock as she came, flooding him with her wetness. She knew he must feel every sweet pull of her cunt, trying to suck his dick into her, and she wasted no time reaching down and aiming him at her spasming hole.

"Ohhh fuck, baby, no," he groaned as she began to slide down onto him. His hands grabbed her hips, stopping her, and she cried out in frustration, feeling just the big head of his cock throbbing inside of her. "No, no, listen, wait… remember, we talked about getting tested before we…"

"Nooooo," she wailed, nearly sobbing against him, biting at his shoulder, desperate to have him. Yes, he'd brought up the subject of diseases and multiple partners and it was all very logical, and at the time Lindsey understood. Now, though, riding up and down against the sweet length of his cock, aching for him inside of her, she didn't care. "Pleeeeeease don't make me stop…"

She felt him giving in, the way his hands eased up on her hips, the deep throb of his cock as he lifted himself, just a little, seeking more heat. It would have happened, she knew it would have—if the damned phone hadn't rung. He tumbled her off of him, hanging onto his unbuckled jeans in one hand and grabbing for the phone, but he was too late. It went to message while Lindsey pulled her top back down and her shorts into place and curled up on the couch hugging one of the pillows.

"Hey, baby, it's Alicia. I'm in town for a few days. I'd *love* to get together, so give me a call, okay?"

Lindsey had lifted her head, incredulous, as some Beyonce wannabe left her number on Zach's answering machine while he zipped his jeans and went to hit "stop" as fast as he could. It was too late, though. She'd got the message—loud and clear.

"That's not what you think," Zach insisted as she pulled on her sandals. "Lindsey, listen, she's—"

"Don't worry about it," Lindsey remembered saying, unchaining and unlocking the apartment door. "At least *somebody* is gonna get fucked this weekend." She hadn't wanted to see his face when she threw the last comment over her shoulder. "Who knows, maybe I will, too."

"Lindsey!"

In her memory, the voice was Zach's calling from the top of the stairs as she tromped down them, but she realized, after a moment, that someone was actually calling her name. Turning, still holding the laundry detergent against her hip and expecting to see her mother waiting impatiently at the end of the aisle, she instead found Brian, his eyes sweeping over her outfit as he stood there, grinning stupidly from ear to ear.

"What do you want?" Lindsey sighed, shifting the detergent to her other hip.

"I dunno." Brian shrugged, still grinning that goofy grin. "I just saw you and thought... you might wanna meet at the tree fort again?"

Lindsey looked at him for a moment, contemplating it. The memory of Zach and the phone call was fresh in her mind and she chewed her lip, seeing the way Brian's eyes moved over her. "What time?"

"Say nine?" He looked at his watch. "I get out of here at eight."

"Okay." She turned and then glanced back. "Just you?"

"Do you want me to invite more?"

"Sure." Lindsey kept going, calling over her shoulder. "The more the merrier."

"All right!" He was already digging his cell phone out of his pocket.

Lindsey saw Mr. Finn again that evening while she was changing in the garden. She flashed him a view from behind when she pulled her short shorts on, winking over the fence as she passed.

"Have a good night," she called.

He shook his head. "You're a bad girl."

"I try!"

She'd expected the same guys as last time—the one she'd fucked again at the pool, Ralph, and maybe the little shy blonde one, too. She doubted Brian had too many other friends he was willing to share with. She didn't know then how she misjudged him.

It wasn't dark when she reached the tree fort—it wouldn't be full dark for another hour—but the light was starting to fade under the canopy of the trees, and it was entirely too quiet for her liking. She expected talking, laughter, anticipatory howls even, a radio perhaps. She could only hear her own breath, fast and light, and the sound of the wind shifting the leaves overhead.

Maybe they hadn't arrived yet. Maybe that was good. She had considered not coming at all, even though she'd said she would. Changing in the garden gave her a little thrill, but the walk didn't have the usual crotch-tingling anticipation. In fact, she felt decidedly uninterested in being there. More than that— she felt sad, and even a little guilty, especially when she thought about Zach.

She was thinking about going home and calling Zach, taking the long way, maybe stopping by 7-11 for a Slurpee, when the cloth slipped over her head from behind, enveloping her in darkness. She knew who it must be, what they were doing—of course, not all of what they intended to do, not by a long shot—so her struggle was expected, but it was also in earnest. She wasn't playing. She didn't want to play this game anymore. Not that it mattered.

"Where's her fucking tits?"

Lindsey shrieked when rough hands pulled her top down, squeezing her breasts hard. Someone was holding her from behind, arms locked around her elbows, and her panicked, heated panting pulled the dark cloth into her mouth again and again. Lindsey used the strength of whoever was holding her to lift herself, aiming her legs in front of her and pistoning them out, hard. She heard a satisfying "Oof!"

"Bitch!" a voice gasped and she shrieked when the backhand came out of nowhere—of course, she couldn't see it coming. It was a hard hit, landing solidly against her temple, making her ears ring with the blow. She even saw stars for a moment and then her lip burst against her teeth like plump fruit, only fat with blood instead of juice, when they hit her again.

"She likes it, I'm telling you!" That was Brian's voice—he was the one holding her. She struggled in his arms, twisting uselessly, tasting copper and swallowing her own blood.

"No!" Her hoarse voice pleaded with them. "Please!"

"That's what she said last time," Brian chuckled, hefting her arms, pulling her in tighter. "I'm telling you, she loves the rough shit."

"Good." The voice she didn't recognize made Lindsey's insides turn cold. "I'm gonna give her plenty of it."

"Not like this," Lindsey gasped as someone pulled the cloth or blindfold or whatever it was up over her mouth and tied it hard behind her head, leaving her bleeding lips free, but she was still unable to see.

"How are we gonna get her up there?" It was another voice Lindsey didn't recognize, rougher than the first, like his throat was filled with gravel or grit.

"I don't want her up there." That was the smooth one—the one who'd backhanded her, she was sure. His voice was smooth and deadly, like a snake. "Hand me that rope."

Lindsey moaned softly as they began to tie her, and she stopped resisting as hands pulled off her shorts and top. They pulled her hands up high, using some sort of tree limb, she was sure, stretching her so far that she had to go up on her tiptoes, losing her sandals in the process. She tried to balance in the dirt, feeling pine needles under her feet as they continued to work around her, pulling, prodding, spreading her legs and securing those, too, with rope. Her arms ached already, but she had a feeling that was going to be the least of her worries in the pain department in the long run.

She tried to think of things to say, a way out of this, to gain control, the upper hand. They had left her mouth free, and she could have talked, but everything that came into her head was a plea, and she knew it was what they wanted—it would only fuel things further—and she was determined, now, not to give them what they wanted. Not until she had to.

"How are we gonna fuck her like that?" Brian sounded truly confused, but Lindsey wasn't at all surprised by the answer.

"I'm not gonna fuck her." Smooth's voice was almost right next to her ear and she startled at his closeness as she heard Gritty laugh on the other side of her. "Not yet, anyway."

"But—"

Lindsey winced at the sound of the blow, hearing Brian cry out, "What the fuck?" He sounded genuinely surprised, but she wasn't surprised at all. She knew their type. The two guys Brian had brought with him tonight would only get off on hurt, not just force, but the mean, sadistic kind of hurt that spilled over from the case of Bud they'd brought with them, but more, it spilled from them like pressure cookers gone too long with something really nasty boiling inside, something unable to contain itself. Brian was just starting to see the overflow. Lindsey knew she would be the brunt of whatever explosion eventually occurred.

"Shut the fuck up, kid." Smooth grabbed the back of Lindsey's head, her hair in his fist, the blindfold tightening to the point of pain. He kissed her, but it wasn't any sort of real kiss—it was just an attempt to bruise her mouth with his, forcing her to cry out as her teeth collided with her lower lip and started the bleeding again. He wanted to hear her and she knew it, trying to keep her pain in with whimpers, trying not to show her fear.

"She's got a nice little cooze." Gritty's fingers— she knew it was him, his voice was on the other side of her—were short and stubby, just as she imagined he was, and probably his little dick, too. They probed between her pussy lips, searching.

"No tits, though." Smooth grabbed them again, twisting, pulling so hard she could feel instant bruises forming. "Might as well cut the damned things off and start over." Gritty laughed, a dark snort and chortle, his fingers still probing between her thighs.

"What do you think, girlie?" The heat of his body felt huge beside her, overpowering, and she felt more than heard a gentle *click* beside her cheek. "Wanna just lose the baby tits and start over again?"

She felt a scream rising from her throat as he scraped the blade-end of a knife gently over her cheek, back and forth, and fought hard against it. There was no one to hear her, she knew, and screaming would just give them what they wanted. She held as still as she could as he drew the knife's edge over her skin, petting her with it, as if he were trying to shave off the soft, downy peach fuzz covering her flesh. When he reached her breasts, he stopped, and Lindsey held her breath, trembling, willing herself not to panic.

"Answer me." His voice remained calm—deadly calm, that same smooth tone.

"Please." Lindsey moaned and tried to make her chest concave as the tip of the knife pressed between them. She felt something wet running down her belly and it was a moment before she realized it was her own blood. Panic rose again, long before she felt the burning pain at the site of the knife-tip grazing her skin, and she knew she was losing it. "I don't know you! I just want to go home, now, okay? I need to... I have to go home and sleep now."

Smooth's chuckle was as smooth as his voice. "You can sleep all you want, sweetheart...when I'm done with you."

I need to go to the moon.

The voice in her head was already distant and she looked up, as if she weren't blindfolded, searching for a glimpse of it through the blackness. She knew the moon would just be rising, and in her mind's eye, she focused there, feeling herself going, going... gone.

Daddy, I fell down.

Her little girl self was cowering somewhere, but she didn't show it. Inside, she was filled with those hitching, uncontrollable sobs, and she saw her father's face, his eyes soft with concern, kissing her to knee to try and make it better. She was afraid of the medicine, afraid of the band-aid, afraid of the pain.

Close your eyes and go to the moon, Lindsey, like we do at night before you go to sleep, and it won't hurt so much.

So she did. She pulled back, away from herself, floating somewhere above it all. And she could see them, somehow she could see it all, the looming shadows moving around her as she strained against the ropes, strung up and helpless. She wanted to scream, but she knew no one would come. No one would believe her. No one ever did. There was no one to protect her and there never would be. There was nothing to do except float, somewhere above it all, watching as they beat her, and when she didn't respond to that, tearing the limbs from branches and using those to bloody her back and legs.

"Shit, man, what's wrong with her?" Gritty smacked her hard across the face, rocking her head back, but Lindsey didn't make a sound. She was far above it, a roar like the sound of the F-16s flying overhead filling her ears, the pain just a dream.

"Is she dead?" That was Brian's voice, shaking, scared. Lindsey wanted to call to him, tell him it was okay, she was okay, but words wouldn't form in her swollen mouth.

"Get her down." Smooth sounded disgusted, very unsatisfied.

The ropes stopped holding her and she collapsed into the dirt like a child's doll. There was a voice in her head, forming words, just one: *Run! Run! Run!* But her body wouldn't cooperate. In her mind, she was running, sprinting down the path, over logs, ignoring the sting of branches against her face, but still she could see herself, limbs bloody and folded beneath her in the dirt as the shadows loomed again.

"Okay, kid, saddle up."

"What?" Brian's voice was still shaking and Lindsey wanted to comfort him, but she still couldn't move.

"You heard me! Get on that bitch and ride her!"

"I—"

Lindsey didn't know what was happening, but gentle hands turned her, the dirt incredibly cool and even soothing against her stinging back and behind. She felt herself coming back into her body and she fought it, but couldn't.

Brian's voice trembled in her ear as he leaned over her, fumbling with the buckle on his jeans. "I'm sorry, I'm so sorry…"

Something flopped between her legs, and she realized he was trying to jam himself into her soft.

"What's the matter with you, fuckhead?" Smooth snorted. "Can't get a fucking hard-on?"

"I—"

"It's okay." Lindsey reached down and found him, limp and wilting in her hand, and she began to stroke him. Her touch was practiced, expert, her thumb rubbing the sensitive glans as she whispered into Brian's ear all the things she knew men loved to hear.

"That's it, baby. I want that hard dick in my wet little cunt. I'm so hot for you. Feel that wet pussy? You want to sink your cock in that hot little hole?"

"Ohhh fuck." Brian shook his head, denying it, but his cock was hardening in her hand.

"She really *does* like it!" Gritty's voice was too close—he was on the ground beside her—and she shrank from the sound.

Brian whispered, "Lindsey, I'm so sorry…"

"Come on," she whispered back, aiming his now-full erection between her legs. "Fuck me. Give them a good show."

"Yeah, that's it…" Smooth's voice was almost a whisper, too, somewhere over her. She could imagine him licking his lips, rubbing his crotch while he watched, getting ready to get it out to stroke it to the live porn show in front of him. "Fuck that cunt!"

She tried to block them out, but she was back in her body now, feeling the length of Brian's cock moving in her, the gentle grunting, his breath coming faster against her ear. The weight of him reminded her how broken she felt, but the pain was, at least, something to concentrate on, and she wondered how bad it really was.

"Suck this, you little whore!" It was Gritty's voice, and she had been right about his short, fat dick. He shoved it between her bruised and swollen lips, and she opened more from self-protection than anything else, letting him slide it back toward her throat. It wasn't long enough to choke her, and for that she was grateful.

"Get up on your knees, kid," Smooth directed. "I wanna watch those baby titties bounce."

Brian shifted his weight, and Lindsey would have sighed in relief if she hadn't had a cock pumping in and out of her mouth. She didn't like how exposed and vulnerable she felt, though, without Brian on top of her, and it wasn't long before Smooth was pinching her nipples and twisting her flesh in his fingers, making her cry out around the thrust of the determined dick in her mouth.

"Ahhh, god," Brian moaned between her thighs, his hips pumping faster. Her blindfold had slipped, and she could see him beneath it, his face screwed up, lips pursed, and if she didn't know it was in pleasure, she might have thought he was in great pain. She also glimpsed her clothes beside her, a flash of white and red, and she closed her fist over them while he fucked her, waiting for it to be over.

"Yeah! Yeah!" Smooth was getting all excited, slapping her tits, pinching her nipples, making her squirm in the dirt. "Make a mess, kid. Come all over the little slut!" Then came the distinctive feel of a hand shuttling up and down the length of a cock against her tits, and since there was one in her mouth and another in her pussy, she knew this dick must belong to

Smooth. He groaned and thrust over her, never letting up in his torture to her breasts. "Uh! Uh! Oh, yeah! Like this, kid! Ohhh yeah! Drown her little baby tits in it!"

Brian moaned and slid out from between her legs, letting loose with hot jets of cum that splashed in wet trails over her belly and cunt. The sight of both of them coming at once must have been too much for Gritty, who began to come in Lindsey's mouth. She spit it out, gagging, and he groaned, aiming his short, spurting cock toward her belly and tits along with the rest of them, covering her with their cum.

"I thought you wanted to fuck her," Brian panted, still sounding so genuinely confused that Lindsey didn't know whether to laugh or cry.

"I wouldn't fuck that shit if you paid me a million dollars." The knee in her side made her gasp, and the pain was so incredible she wondered if he'd broken her rib.

Still, Lindsey knew there wasn't much time. Their cocks were wet and growing limp, and this might be her only chance before the real meanness began. And she knew it was coming—it was just a matter of time. The feel of the clothes balled in her fist, the little short shorts and tube top, is what got her moving. Brian was fumbling with his jeans between her legs and she rolled to her side—toward Gritty, not Smooth—and bolted.

"Fuck!" Smooth hadn't expected her to be so fast, she knew from the surprise in his voice, but she was, in spite of the pain, incredibly quick. She pulled the blindfold off, throwing it behind her as she ran down the path. Her lungs ached and the ground bit at her feet, but she didn't pay any attention. They were behind her, coming for her, and she had to keep going.

"Going somewhere, hot stuff?" He grabbed her hair, yanking it hard and stopping her short. Gritty panted up behind him, and Lindsey turned her face up toward them both, on her knees now, panting with her effort to get away.

Smooth was just as smooth as she'd imagined, older, his tanned, lined face twisted into a sneer. His hair was bleach blonde and spiked, though, not the dark she'd imagined, and he looked strangely like he was wearing a halo as she stared up at him. Gritty bent over, panting, hands resting on his knobby, hairy knees. His pants were completely off, and his belly hung almost low enough to hide his softening dick.

"Not done with you, yet." Smooth had his jeans on, but they were still undone, and he brought her face toward his crotch, rubbing it there, the teeth of his zipper raking her lips, making her wince.

"I saw you both." It was all she said before she brought her head down and then up hard into his crotch, thanking god for all those years of learning how to head-butt a soccer ball. Smooth went down in a hissing, writhing heap, and she was gone again, off running, finally, for real this time and not in her mind, her body finally cooperating.

She didn't stop until she reached the edge of the path, glancing behind her to make sure they weren't following. Then she pulled her clothes quickly on, although she knew they didn't cover the mess she was. Thank god it was nearly dark, now, and she limped home as the moon started to rise, an orange blaze over her shoulder.

She didn't make a garden stop to change back into her regular clothes. Instead, she tried to sneak quietly up the back stairs to her room. Her mother's car was gone, but her stepfather's was in the driveway, and that meant she would have to be extra careful.

Breathing a sigh of relief, she shut her door behind her and leaned against it, closing her eyes. Everything hurt—it even hurt to breathe—but she was home, safe in her own room. That, at least—

"You little slut."

Lindsey's eyes flew open at the sound of his voice. Her stepfather was sitting on her bed, and the sight of her journals open in a heap around him made her stomach sink to her knees. They had been hidden in the wall, behind a loose piece of paneling. She thought they would never find them...

"If your mother saw these, you know what would happen."

If she could have taken a step back, she would have, but the door was solid behind her, barring the way. He was coming for her, towering over her, and she shrank down into a ball on the floor, covering her head with her arms.

"We're going to burn them." He grabbed her by the hair, pulling her up, and Lindsey flashed back to the woods and fought the urge to scream. "And you are never..." He shook her, holding her shoulders now, his fingers digging into the tender, broken flesh of her back. "...ever, *ever* going to do something like that again!"

Something inside of her broke open, spilling out in hot waves as she stared at him. "What? What did I do?"

He shook her, his face inches from hers, teeth clenched so tightly it was hard to understand him through the sneer. "You know just what you did, you teasing little whore!"

"It wasn't me!" Lindsey shook her head, incredulous. "It was you! *You!*"

"You asked for it." He dropped his hands from her and went over to the bed and started throwing her journals into a box. He was going to burn them, as if he could rid himself of her and everything that had happened, sweep it away and pretend it never existed.

"Maybe I've deserved every horrible thing you've ever done to me." Her voice shook as she watched him stacking the scarred and pained words of her adolescence into a cardboard box. "I just hope it was worth it. Did it make you feel like a man—fucking your twelve-year-old stepdaughter?"

He turned to her, his face red with anger at the words, but Lindsey didn't stop. "Oh right, I'm not supposed to talk about it—and who would believe a little slut like me, anyway? Certainly not my own mother. Not after the stories you told about me."

Lindsey paused to take a shaky breath, remembering the slow erosion that had happened between her and her mother over the years as he started to harp on Lindsey about her clothes, her developing body. "I wasn't a slut until you made me one... going on and on about all the boys I'd fucked at the ripe old age of twelve... when the truth was, the only one who ever touched me was *you!*"

"Shut up!" He came toward her, his posture threatening, but she couldn't stop. Something had cracked open in her tonight. Maybe it had happened in the woods, when they tied her up, forced her down, worked her cunt as if that was all she was, holes to be filled, something to be used and tossed away. It had begun seeping out then, like the blood from her lip, but now it broke open, a flood.

Like the night the moon was in my window...

She remembered that in a flood, too, a deluge, and the memory tasted bitter, like copper on her tongue. Even that memory was unsafe. It came in a flood, like the blood between her legs had flowed when he forced himself on her, in her, and she couldn't do anything but endure. The moon had floated in a square patch of window, and she had gone away then—*I fell down, Daddy*—all the way to the moon, just like she had earlier tonight.

"You knew I was a virgin!" Lindsey screamed, the ache in her chest bursting as she sobbed, not wanting to but remembering everything she'd been hiding, covering, holding back—everything she had poured into those journals. "And you left me... in all that blood... so much blood..."

Her voice cracked and she spat the last at him. "I had to throw the sheets away and turn my mattress over so my own mother wouldn't see what you'd done to me!"

Lindsey grabbed the edge of the bed and shoved it toward the wall, tipping the twin mattress up, revealing the darkened stain underneath as it slid off the box spring. She pointed to it, trembling, remembering how she had scrubbed and scrubbed, tears and snot mixing with the blood on the mattress, wishing she could just melt away, erase herself, until she became transparent.

"Get out!" He reached past her for the doorknob, his voice shaking. "I want you out of my house."

"Oh, I have no intention of staying." Lindsey turned to go, and they both saw her mother standing just outside the door, hand raised as if to knock, her face pale, eyes wide.

Lindsey just brushed past her, not saying a word. Her whole body ached as if it was on fire, beaten, broken, but somehow she felt lighter as she walked, barefoot, down the street, looking for the nearest pay phone where she would call Zach and ask him to come for her. Maybe, she whispered to the rising moon, just maybe, there was finally someone in the world who might believe her.

Chapter Eight

She wouldn't have done it for anyone else, and her eyes sought Zach's after every question. Yet she still found the words sticking in her throat as the officer scribbled on her pad, trying to look unbiased and nonjudgmental. Lindsey didn't think she was doing a very good job, and she thought sending a woman was just cheap—as if she would feel more comfortable with a female? Not likely.

"So, did you know any of your assailants?"

Lindsey cleared her throat. "I…no." It was the first time she'd lied, and the first time she didn't lift her eyes to Zach's.

"And you obviously resisted, fought back, told them no?"

"Yes." She traced the top edge of the thin hospital sheet covering the hospital gown the nurse insisted she wear. Her voice was almost inaudible, but she couldn't seem to make it any stronger. "But I always tell them no."

"What?" The detective leaned in, tucking a stray blonde hair from her ponytail behind her ear. "What was that?"

"I always say no." Lindsey still didn't look up, feeling something burning in her throat, but she went on. "It's a game. It's a thing. I just…I like to say no, and have them, you know, do it anyway."

She felt their eyes on her and didn't want to look up and see their faces—especially Zach. She half-expected him to get up and go, right then. The silence seemed to stretch forever, and then, finally, the detective spoke again.

"How are they supposed to know the difference?"

"I don't know." Lindsey shrugged. "Does it matter?"

"Did you have an agreement with these men? Did they know that your 'no' meant yes?"

Lindsey thought of Brian—of all of them, he was the only one who really knew the game. Had he told the new ones, the others? She didn't know, but figured he must have. His continuous apology, both verbal and non, told her that much. They knew the game, but when her "no" had turned insistent, when even Brian knew she didn't want to play the game anymore, the others had gone on.

She remembered Smooth, the look in his eyes. He didn't care about the game—he didn't want her to like it, and most especially, he didn't want her to be in control. Everything he did made it clear she was helpless, powerless before him. He'd known she didn't want what they were dishing out, that her "no" had really meant "no."

But there was no way to tell the detective that. How could she possibly defend herself? And if she told this woman there *was* some sort of agreement, she would have to admit knowing Brian, tell them about her encounters with him before, even though the rest of them had been strangers to her. She remembered the tears in Brian's eyes, the apology there, and knew she couldn't.

"No…" Lindsey sighed. "It was just a game I played in my head."

The detective, who had kept her distance the whole time, business-like, writing in her little note pad, took a step toward the bed. Lindsey flinched, only able to bring her eyes up to the level of the woman's badge.

"That's a dangerous game, Lindsey."

She snorted, finally looking at the woman's face through half-closed eyes—she couldn't open them any further, and they were still crusted with blood. "Obviously."

"We'll have a sketch artist contact you and I want you to look through our mugshots." The blonde—her name, officer Deborah Bills, was embroidered on her uniform pocket, and Lindsey wondered for a moment if the woman had done it herself—closed her notebook and tucked it away into that pocket for safekeeping. "If you can identify the suspects and there is enough evidence to charge them, you'll be asked to testify."

The thought made Lindsey's stomach drop, but she just nodded. "Can I go home now?"

"You'll have to talk to the doctor about that." The officer took a card from a holder and put it on the adjustable hospital bedside table. "This has my number on it. If you've forgotten anything, or there's something new you have to say, give me a call."

The doctor insisted she stay, but Lindsey signed herself out AMA. "I'm eighteen. I can do that, right?"

The doc was a short Asian woman with a cruel mouth that twisted when she was mad—like now—but kind eyes, and she looked like she wanted to say, "No," but she didn't. "Technically, yes."

Zach spoke up then for the first time in what felt like hours. "I can take care of her, if she wants to go."

The Asian doc looked him up and down for a moment, and finally even her mouth softened with a resigned sigh. "She's had a good deal of head trauma. Check her often during the night, look at her pupils…"

Lindsey ignored the rest, hopping off the bed like a five-year-old who just got her own way and, after checking one last time with the doc, went to take a shower. It was more painful that she would have believed, in more ways than one. The hot water over her lacerated back and legs hit her like sharp needles, and anywhere she touched herself with the soap felt bruised and broken. She didn't even attempt to wash the purple and, in some places, near-black nubs of her breasts, just let the suds from her shampoo drip down her body—and that burned, too, in the little cuts and nicks along her abdomen and the front of her thighs.

She stood there a long time in the heat, letting the water massage her front, washing away the dried residue of their cum. Her memory was too clear and bright, even if it only came in flashes, like someone taking photos at night. She saw herself, still, outside of herself, hanging suspended, beaten, aching, bleeding. *Flash.* A slim girl spread flat in the pine needles and dirt, three men kneeling over her, working their way into her, on her, in one way or another. *Flash.* Brian's face an apology, his trembling hands gripping her hips. *Flash.* Running, desperate, the birch trees like negatives in the growing darkness. *Flash.* Her stepfather, looming. *Flash.* A blood stained mattress, the darkness spread like a question mark, or a crescent moon. *Flash.* Zach's stunned face, the twist from disbelief to anger, his hands gentle, his words soft.

She cried then, turning the water salt, shoving a washcloth into her mouth to muffle her sobs. Zach was right outside the door, and listening, she was sure of it. There was only so much pain one man could stand, she reasoned, as she bent over double, retching, nothing in her stomach, but vomiting anyway, as if she could rid herself of every memory but the last.

Finally, she stood, paying special attention to the area between her legs then, using one of the harsh, bleached hospital washcloths laved with soap to scrub herself clean. Her whole body felt raw as she used the rough, stingy towels to dry off and realized she didn't have any clothes to put on, the hospital gown just a blood-stained ball on the floor.

"Zach?" Poking her head out the door, she spoke in a stage whisper, looking around for the doc, but she was gone. "I don't have anything to wear."

He looked up from where he was sitting, head in hands, in the chair next to the bed. "She left you something. I guess they...they keep stuff on hand for when..." He let his words trail off, but the sentence finished itself in her head, anyway. *"For when women get raped."* Lindsey held out her hand, thinking about the sentence he hadn't wanted to finish, and he put a bag into it.

Raped. And so, she had been. *Wouldn't be the first time*, she mused, digging through the bag. Sweatpants, bright pink, size large—she was going to swim in them—and a t-shirt with a logo she recognized from another business-sized card sitting on the table out there in her hospital room. *Turning Point.* It was the place that other woman was from, the one who said she was a social worker, an advocate. Lindsey had dispatched her pretty quickly, she remembered, pulling the clothes on, tying a knot in the sweats on the side so they would stay up.

"Get out," Lindsey had insisted, pointing toward the door in case the young social worker had missed the way. "I don't want to talk to you."

The dark-haired woman had persisted for a few minutes, trying to explain her role. "I'm just here as a friend, really," she explained. "Someone you can talk to."

"What part of 'I don't want to talk to you' didn't you understand, lady?"

Lindsey had submitted to the examination, the questions from the nurse, the doctor, demanding in spite of their objections that Zach stay by her side—she squeezed his hand the whole time—not because she wanted to, or even thought it was necessary, but because he had insisted she report it. But this, this woman claiming she just wanted "to talk"—that affront was just one step too far.

She'd heard the woman whispering with the cop in the hallway, but hadn't seen her again after she'd left her business card.

"Ready to go home?" Zach looked up when she came out of the bathroom, still tugging up the sweats.

Home. She didn't have a home anymore, she remembered. She couldn't ever go back there again. Part of her was gleeful at the thought, but another part ached with a loss that made no logical sense at all. Zach slipped his arm around her waist, tucking her discharge papers into his back pocket. She made her best effort not to wince at the pain as they made their way down the hospital hallway, ignoring the eyes of the cop, who was still filling out paperwork at the desk and talking to the social worker Lindsey had kicked out of her room.

"It's gonna be okay, baby," Zach murmured, pushing the button for the elevator, his hand moving up to cup the back of her neck, massaging with his thumb.

She nodded, stepping in as the doors opened, and couldn't believe how much she wanted to trust him.

* * * *

"I should have stayed at the hospital!" Lindsey groaned as Zach turned off the alarm and flipped on the light next to the bed for the thousandth time that night.

"Open your eyes," he insisted, pulling her arm from across them.

She sighed, blinking at the brightness, shaking off the dream she'd been in the middle of—something about swallowing small blue marbles, one after another, until she felt impossibly full. His gaze moved over her face, flickering between each of her eyes in studied concentration.

"Okay," he said finally, giving her a reluctant nod. "We can go back to sleep."

"Ha." She stuck her tongue out at him. "Aren't you supposed to heal best while sleeping? I don't think getting up every two hours constitutes sleeping!"

"Sorry, baby." His smile was infuriating as he reached for the light switch. "At least we don't have to get up in the morning."

"You're worse than any nurse," Lindsey muttered, yanking the sheet up over her shoulder and turning away from him. The weekend, she realized—no school for her, no work for him. But what about Monday? What then? Would everyone know what had happened? Her reputation had been in shreds for years, so she didn't care a bit about that, but whatever she'd done before had been her choice, she reasoned. This time…

"You cold?" Zach pulled the comforter up to join the sheet at her neckline when she shivered.

"No." She winced at the pain of his touch on her tender back. "Yes. I don't know."

He lowered his head to touch hers in the darkness, kissing the top of her ear. "I wish…"

"Don't say it." She didn't think she could stand another ounce of kindness or pity.

Zach sighed, his breath warm on her neck. "I don't think I have the words, anyway."

"Good."

He feathered kisses over the back of her neck, pushing her long hair out of his way. "Sleep…"

"I was," she sighed as he settled in behind her, pressing his chest to her back, forgetting, she knew, but she couldn't help her gasp of pain at the sudden pressure.

"Ah damn!" He moved back a little, his big hand resting on her hip. "Oh damnit, Lindsey. Damn them!"

His sudden change, the vehement anger in his tone, startled her. The Zach she knew didn't get angry, not really. The hand moving over her hip shook, and she knew it was trembling with rage.

"I could kill them." He whispered it under the cover of the darkness, as if he'd been afraid to speak the words aloud before, in the light, with all its possibilities. "With my bare hands."

She believed him. "It was my own fault."

"No." His grip tightened, and his hand would have made a fist if he hadn't been squeezing her hip. "I don't care what you said about the little games you play—*played*," he made his insistence on past tense perfectly clear, "with these guys." His voice broke and she heard nothing but his breath, harsh and uneven, for a moment. "No one deserves what happened to you. You didn't do this to yourself, Lindsey. You didn't beat your back into a bloody pulp, or…or…"

It was like he couldn't make any more words. She gave a strangled little laugh that sounded more like a sob to her ears. "Didn't I?"

"No," he murmured, pulling the sheet aside, exposing her back to the air. "Oh my god, no, sweetheart, no..." His lips moved over her back, kissing the wounds there. The deeper ones he had carefully bandaged before they'd gone to bed, but there were too many to cover completely, and it was the shallow ones he kissed now, over and over. It reminded her of those few memories she had of her father, of falling down and him putting on the Band-Aid, kissing it and making it all better. "Please don't believe it. Not for a minute. You didn't ask for this. It's not your fault."

She didn't believe it—couldn't—and she cringed away, rolling to her belly and clutching the pillow. He didn't stop touching her, his fingers grazing lightly, cautious, as if he were petting a shy animal, his lips murmuring words against her back, and he kept on whispering those awful, painful words.

"I know you're hurting." His breath was too warm, too human, too comforting. It made her want to cry and she fought it—hard. "God, baby, I could tell from the first minute I saw you. It shouldn't be possible for a girl your size to be carrying around so much pain."

"No," she choked, begging him to stop, knowing he wouldn't. This was worse, his tenderness, his kind words, worse than the rape, worse than anything.

"I just want to love you." His forehead pressed against her lower back, and the sting she felt there was the salt of his tears. That realization broke her—Zach, crying, in pain—and all she wanted to do was curl into a ball and die.

"I don't deserve you." She sobbed against the pillow, the dam breaking, her body shaking with it. "I don't deserve this."

"Oh, baby." Zach moved in beside her, taking her, fighting, into his arms. She tried to resist, shaking her head, pushing back, but he was too strong for her. "Please," he murmured into her hair as she began to give, letting him hold her. "Let me love you. Just let me love you."

"I can't." Her strangled cry muffled itself against his chest, and he rocked her, back and forth, into a bed covers cocoon in the dark. "You don't understand."

"I don't care." He tucked her head under his chin, as if he could get her even closer. "Lindsey, I know more than you think I do. And I don't care. Baby, I don't care what you've done, how many other guys you've been with, the lengths you've gone to...just to hurt yourself." She tried to make herself smaller against him, as if she could hide from his words.

"God, baby, you're so full of that spite." His words made her feel cold, achy, as if she had the flu. "Watching you do this to yourself...it's like seeing you eat rat poison, but you think you're hurting someone else, don't you? You'll show them, right?" He squeezed her tighter when she snorted and nodded through her tears. "And all the while you're just killing *yourself...*"

"I know." She drew a shuddering breath. "But I don't care."

He sighed, kissing the top of her head. "Because if no one else cares...why should you?"

She nodded, holding back a full-blown sob, her throat closing off any words.

"*I* care, Linds." He cupped her face in his hands, kissing her wet cheeks. "I love you. Do you hear me? *I love you.*"

Burying her face against his chest, she gave a deep, shuddering sigh, sliding her hand down over the hard, flat surface of his belly, reaching under the sheet to find his cock, soft in a nest of dark, kinky hair.

"Lindsey!" Zach jumped, startled, at her touch. "Oh, baby, no, no…" He took her hand, pulling it up to his waist, wrapping it around him. "It's so not about that."

"It's always about that!" she choked, trying to push him away, but he wouldn't let her. Instead, he held on, rocking, until sobs racked her body, trembling them both. It was a while—to Lindsey, it felt like forever—before they subsided into little hitching noises, the same kind she used to get when she was very small and had been crying a long, long time. Zach kissed the top of her head, using the sheet to wipe the tears from her face, his chest.

"He raped me," she whispered, the words lifting a weight in her chest like an anvil.

"I know, baby, I know," he crooned, stroking her. "I'm so sorry…"

"My stepfather. When I was twelve."

His silence stretched until he managed a breathy, strangled, "Oh…god…" in response, his arms tightening around her.

"I had never even kissed a boy before." The words, once begun, seemed to form themselves.

"Oh Christ."

"There was blood everywhere." She shuddered. "And I tried to clean it—he told me to, before my mother got home. I tried…" She sighed, remembering. The memory wasn't far away, like it usually was—the circle-face of the moon through a pane of glass—instead it was close, bright, painful. She wanted to push it away and found she couldn't. "He was always like that. I couldn't ever do anything right with him. It never mattered what it was. I wasn't ever good enough."

"Oh my god, Lindsey," Zach's voice cracked and she could feel how tense his muscles were, felt his jaw clench as he tucked her head under his chin. The words came and came, spilling out of her mouth, a fountain of pain, and he listened, mostly quiet, his jaw working, as she told him everything.

"I remembered…" She tried to swallow the memory, but she couldn't. It hurt more than any of the others. "When I was little-little and I'd fall down and skin my knee…I remembered my father, putting on that spray stuff that hurt and telling me to go to the moon…"

"The moon?"

"It was something we did…" She smiled through her tears, remembering her chubby little girl finger, pointing at the glass. "At night, he would show me the moon out my window before he put me to bed…so whenever I was hurt, he'd try to distract me, tell me to remember the moon…think about the moon…"

Zach nodded, just holding her.

"I think I got to the point where I became the moon," she whispered, closing her eyes. She could see it, tucked neatly into one square pane of glass. "I went to the moon whenever he touched me, Zach. I went away. Whenever anyone touches me, that's where I go. And tonight…I went there, too. I felt like I swallowed the moon tonight, and it burned…"

"Oh baby…" He gave a deep, shaky sigh, swallowing hard. "Can I ask…what about your mother?"

"I tried...once." Lindsey shook her head. "She wouldn't listen. She didn't want to know." Her lip trembled and she pulled the comforter tighter around her. "She always loved him more than she ever loved me."

"Oh no..." His denial didn't make it not true, and she blinked back more tears.

"And after that...I just wanted someone to pick me up and tell me it was going to be okay, you know?" She felt him nodding. "But there was never...anyone. And it felt like...like I just kept falling down...over and over...and there was no one there..."

"To catch you?"

She nodded her assent, her throat closed tight.

"I promise you..." Zach's voice was hard, but his hands, cupping her face, were tender. "No one is ever going to hurt you again. And I will always, always be there to catch you, Lindsey."

She wanted to deny his words, to tell him she didn't need him—she didn't need anyone—but that part of her was far away now. He'd managed to find a way into the biggest, most secret part of herself, and she couldn't push him away anymore.

"I don't care how hard or how far you fall," he murmured, kissing her wet eyelids, her cheeks, her lips. "I promise I will be there to catch you."

"I'm sorry," she choked, wrapping her arms around his neck, pressing against him. "I'm so sorry. I love you so much, and I am so, so..."

His kiss stopped her, his mouth hard, too hard, and she cried out. He stopped, panting, and she felt the anger in him. "No, I'm the one who's sorry." He sighed, his fingers moving over her sore, tender lips. "I'm sorry all of that happened to you. I'm sorry you think it was your fault, that you deserved..." He shook his head, swallowing the words. "Lindsey, if I could take it back...if I could get my hands on him in a dark alley somewhere..."

"It doesn't matter," she murmured, throwing a leg over his and snuggling in closer. "None of it matters anymore. I have you now...I have someone, a place to be, to feel safe."

"Oh damnit..." His arms tightened again. "This is so not the right time to tell you this..."

Her head came up sharply, her heart thudding. "Tell me what?"

"...I'm leaving." He winced when she gasped, sounding as if she'd been punched. "I'm being deployed to Iraq."

"Again?" She frowned, feeling indignant. *Just how much time can one man serve for his country?* she thought selfishly.

He sighed. "I go when they tell me to go, baby."

"I don't want you to go." She pouted, trying to imagine her life without him, and found it more than a little difficult.

"And I don't want to go." He leaned back on his pillow, throwing an arm over his head, and stared up at the ceiling.

She approached him cautiously. "You can't get out of it?"

"You can't tell the U.S. Navy no, sweetheart." The flash of his smile gleamed in the dark. "But here's the thing..." He sat up on his elbow, earnest now. "I want you to stay here. Stay here and wait for me."

"Wait?" The word felt weighted in her mouth.

"You're graduating in a few weeks. I'll probably be gone through the summer, no more..."

The whole summer? She sighed. "When are you going?"

"June twenty-sixth."

"So soon?" She heard the whine in her voice and tried to curb it. That was only a few weeks after graduation.

"I'm sorry." He leaned back again, this time throwing his arm over his eyes. "It's terrible timing."

They were quiet for a while. Lindsey watched him, his chest rising and falling, and wondered what he was thinking. "I don't want to stay here without you," she said finally. "This is...this is your home, not mine. I don't belong here."

"Yes you do," he insisted, up on his elbow again. His eyes flashed in the dimness. "Want me to prove it? We'll go the justice of the peace tomorrow."

She laughed, incredulous. "Was that a proposal?"

"Yeah," he said, serious, reaching out for her hand. His swallowed hers as he squeezed and then pressed her palm to his lips. "Yeah, it was. Lindsey, will you marry me?"

Her heart soared, but she tried to make light of it, still. She snorted and gave him a shove. "A shotgun wedding?"

She heard him grinning. "Well, for it to be a *real* shotgun wedding, you'd have to be pregnant... not that I'd object." His hand moved over the smooth, flat expanse of her belly, but she pushed him away, sitting up and swinging her legs over the side of the bed.

"Where are you going?" His hand moved to encircle her wrist.

"I don't know," she whispered, closing her eyes. "Zach...I can't get pregnant. Not anymore."

He sat up then, too, moving in behind her. She leaned her head back against his chest and told him her last, biggest secret. "He made me get an abortion after that first time." She felt him stiffen, but she went on anyway, needing to tell someone, needing to tell *him*. "And then, you know, he got me the pill. But I stopped taking them." She laughed in the dark, remembering how angry, how defiant, how ridiculously naive she had been. "I thought maybe, if I had a baby, my mom would have to..."

"Oh Jesus." He rested his forehead against her hair.

"But it's never happened." She shrugged. She had stopped worrying about it a long time ago. What kind of mother would she ever be, after all, she reasoned. Her own mother had been a terrible mother. And her grandmother—she was the only one who had ever defended her. Her intentions were good—but her sentiments misguided. Her grandmother had hit the tree but missed the target, not quite understanding the motivation behind her granddaughter's acting out. When Lindsey's mother had complained about her daughter's behavior, the way she dressed, Lindsey's grandmother had turned to her granddaughter, patted her hand, and whispered so only she could hear, "Don't worry, dear—a hussy is just a woman with the morals of a man." But she'd died two years ago and now Lindsey had no one at all.

Except now she had Zach.

"All this time," Lindsey went on. "I've never gotten pregnant. And I haven't exactly been careful."

"Oh, baby I'm so sorry…" He wrapped his arms around her waist, pulling her into his lap, her back against his chest, rocking her. "It doesn't matter. I love you. *You.* Do you get that?"

She nodded. She did get it—for the first time, maybe ever. Turning in his arms, she straddled him, up on her knees, to give him a long, tender kiss. She felt him smile against her lips.

"Well the good news is the hospital says I'm clean," she whispered into his ear. "Not even one STD. You know what that means?"

He chuckled. "Is that a yes?"

"Oh yes," she agreed, wiggling in his lap.

"Not *that*." He laughed, pulling her back into bed, covering them both. "*That* can wait."

"To what, then?" she teased. "Your romantic proposal?"

"What else?" He snorted.

She hesitated, biting her lip. "It's a definite maybe."

"Well then you better sleep on it some more." He squeezed his arm around her shoulder as she snuggled up and rested her head on his chest. "My alarm's going to go off in another hour so I can check on you."

She groaned, rolling her eyes before closing them and drifting almost immediately into the soundest sleep she could ever remember.

Chapter Nine

School wasn't as bad as she thought it was going to be, when she went back a week later, after Zach deemed her "healed"—at least, on the outside—although teachers and students alike remarked on Lindsey's sudden, subdued nature. She also heard them talking behind her back about the sudden appearance of jeans without holes ripped through in the seat and tops that actually covered her midriff.

They'd gone back to her house briefly to gather some of her clothes and things—she made sure both cars were gone before they chanced it—but after reviewing the wardrobe she'd chosen to throw into the big white garbage bag they carried out to the Camaro, Zach insisted on taking her to the mall to do some shopping. And when she went, out of habit, to look for a tube top to wear to school that first day, she couldn't even find one in the drawers Zach had cleared for her to use—her new clothes were folded neatly, button-down shirts and crisp new jeans—but all of her old clothes had disappeared.

Zach, of course, feigned innocence, even when she pummeled his back with her fists and pinched his sides, insisting, "You do so know where they are!" He just laughed, shrugged, and gathered her up, still fighting, to kiss her quiet.

So she felt like a complete geek that first day, and even considered ripping out the seat of her jeans—but the guilt of knowing how much Zach had charged on his credit card for their little shopping trip kept her from actually taking scissors from the office to the bathroom with her to go through with her little plan. She even resisted the temptation to unbutton the bottom of her shirt and tie it up high under her breasts.

Instead, she sat quietly in her seat and pretended she was impervious to the stares and the whispers and the double-takes, even from the teachers. There was only another week left of school, anyway. For Zach, she could endure that long. That's what she told herself, and when she walked home every day—his apartment was in easy walking distance from school—letting herself in with the key he'd had made at the local hardware store and even starting dinner before he got home. She knew just from the light, easy way she could breathe, the absence of dread, that it was true.

The only thing looming was Zach's upcoming deployment, and she tried her best not to think about it. That, and the nightmares, which had started after that first night and had continued at least once a night, since. Sometimes she woke him with her panic and he would hold her, but mostly she trembled beside him in the dark, eyes wide, the sheets wet with her sweat, staring up at the ceiling and remembering while he slept beside her, oblivious. If Zach had known, he would have been angry, of course, and insisted she wake him. But she wouldn't. If nothing else, she had learned to keep things to herself.

Although, with Zach, that talent was fading—keeping things from him was getting harder and harder. Her emotions seemed to spill over when he was around, no matter what she did. Like when they saw Brian in the Sav-Way while they were grocery shopping.

"So what do you want for graduation?" Zach asked, taking out the powdered donuts she'd put into the basket and replacing them with a loaf of wheat bread.

Lindsey sighed, eyeing the little chocolate ones instead. "A diploma."

"Don't even think about it." He took the donut box from the hand behind her back, putting them back on the shelf. "I meant besides a diploma."

She followed him down the aisle with a shrug. "I don't know. Got another Camaro lying around?"

He snorted, steering the cart around the corner. "Okay, something bigger than a diploma, but smaller than a Camaro."

Lindsey didn't really hear him. Brian was stocking laundry detergent on the end cap, his head down as he moved the inventory from box to shelf. He hadn't seen her, but she knew he would the minute he glanced up. Zach steered the cart around him, apologizing, and she told herself to move, to follow, to pretend, but her body was frozen in place. She didn't know how they'd avoided each other so far—her computer lab was right next to his English class—but they had. Until now.

"Lindsey?" Zach called her name, and the sound of it brought Brian's head up like a shot, his eyes wide. Zach's face scrunched in concern at her expression, but she couldn't hide it, her gaze dipping down to meet Brian's startled one.

"Hi, Brian." She couldn't think of anything else to say.

"Hi." His response came in almost a whisper, his face paling even more as Zach maneuvered the cart back toward them.

"Someone you know?" Zach inquired, his smile tight as he glanced down at the kid in the red vest stocking shelves. Lindsey didn't have any idea what to say.

"From school." Brian stood quickly—the top of his head didn't even come to Zach's shoulder—and held out a hand to Zach, who shook it. "I'm Brian. Lindsey and I had chem together last year."

"Right," Lindsey agreed with a nod, noting Zach's preoccupied and calculating expression. She didn't want to give him that much time to think about it. "See you Monday?"

"Sure." Brian kept sneaking looks up at Zach, and he looked more than a little scared. Lindsey wondered if she had a similar look on her face—she felt like she did, and like Brian, she just couldn't help it. "See ya Monday."

Lindsey slipped between them and tugged at the front edge of the cart, leading Zach toward the next aisle—frozen foods, including ice cream, the perfect distraction.

"Moose Tracks?" She opened one of the glass doors, the cool blast of air over her too-warm face a relief. She grabbed a quart of ice cream, holding it up for Zach to see. "Please? Pretty please?"

"That's Neapolitan." Zach took it from her, putting it back on the shelf and grabbing a carton with antlers on it. "What was that about?"

"Must have been having bad flashbacks to elementary school birthday parties," she joked, tugging on the cart again.

"Not the ice cream—that kid back there." Zach's grip on the cart now made it impossible to move.

She sighed, giving up the tug of war, and told him part of the truth. "Just a guy I used to hang out with…before."

"Hang out?" He raised his eyebrows, already knowing.

She rolled her eyes, taking advantage of the moment to tug the cart again. "Don't make me say it, okay?"

He gave in, moving along with the cart. "You sure that's all?"

"Waffles!" Lindsey pulled Eggos out of the freezer with a grin, another distraction.

Zach put them back. "If you want waffles, I'll make you *real* waffles."

"You promise?"

He nudged her with the cart. "How about waffles on graduation day?"

"I have to wait a week for waffles?" She pouted.

"Sometimes the best things are worth waiting for."

She didn't respond to that, but she flushed, accepting the kiss he put on the top of her head as he piled the cart with frozen vegetables and then headed toward the checkout. Lindsey snuck a pack of gum and a box of Tic-Tacs onto the conveyor belt and Zach didn't notice until the last second, when the cashier, a blonde with a nose ring, held it up and asked, "Do you want these left out?"

"Thanks!" Lindsey snagged them, giving Zach a grin before slipping them into her jeans pocket. He shook his head, but forked over his credit card without any reprimand and signed his name in a quick scrawl.

"Quarter." She held out her hand as they neared the machines, their fat glass jars revealing all sorts of cheap treasure, their red-painted tops screaming, "Stop here!"

Zach dug into his front jeans pocket, pulling out the required coin. "Which one this time?"

"Let's try fancy jewelry." Lindsey slid the quarter into the slot and turned the knob, hearing the gears inside click, loving the sound of the little plastic tub hitting the metal door.

"Wait a minute." He pressed his hand against hers as she reached for the metal flap, holding it there. "I want to tell you something."

The look on his face made her heart thud faster. "What?"

"I love you." His eyes softened as he studied her, looking up at him puzzled as carts pushed by, letting in the heat of the summer to compete with the store's air conditioning with every pneumatic swing. "I don't care who you've been with. I don't care about anything that happened before. You know that, right?"

She nodded, still not quite believing it could be true, but wanting to—desperately wanting to.

"But I don't want you to be with anyone else but me anymore, Lindsey." His mouth tightened for a moment and she knew he was thinking about Brian. God, if he knew the truth…she blinked the thought away, looking up at him. He was serious now. "I'm going to be gone for months, and I want to trust you. I want to know you're not going to run off to have a fling with some guy, just because you start feeling bad about yourself."

Her throat tightened and she blinked at him, unable to respond.

"I want you to be mine, baby." He touched her cheek, rubbing his thumb over her jaw line. "Forever. Can you do that? Will you do that?"

"Oh Zach." Her eyes filled with tears. Then he did something more than a little surprising. He sank to one knee on the grocery store tile in front of her. Panicked, she looked around to see who was looking, noting the indulgent smile of a woman with a fat little toddler in her cart as she passed by. Lindsey stage-whispered to him, "What are you doing?"

"If there's not a ring in here, I'm going to feel like a real idiot." He grinned, lifting up the metal flap on the machine. A clear plastic tub with a blue cap dropped into his hand. He popped the top off and pulled out the ring inside—it was, indeed, a ring, quite apropos, with two connected silver hearts squeezed together in the center. "We're in luck."

"Oh my god." Lindsey grinned back at him and bit her lip as he held it up.

"Lindsey, will you marry me?"

There was a crowd gathering now—the mother with the toddler had looked back and caught on to what was happening and stopped in the doorway, blocking the exit. Carts were backing up behind her, and they were all watching. Lindsey's face burned, but tears stung her eyes as she flung her arms around his neck.

"Yes," she whispered against his ear, trying hard not to cry in the middle of the grocery store. "I'm all yours."

He grinned up at her, and she couldn't help laughing at his goofy expression—he knew it was silly, a proposal with a fake ring in the middle of Sav-Way— but Zach's hand actually shook as he slid the silver ring onto the appropriate finger, and she knew it wasn't a joke. Not really. The look in his eyes told her that. He really loved her, he wanted her, and he was willing to claim her.

"She said yes?" the woman with the toddler called. She was grinning, too.

Lindsey nodded. "Yes!" she called back as Zach stood and pulled her into his arms, kissing her hard in front of everyone. That's when they all started cheering, and she laughed through her tears, looking over to see the little girl in the cart, clapping along with everyone else, but looking bewildered. Lindsey knew just how she felt.

There were various congratulations as the line began to move again, and carts filed out of the store. Lindsey didn't say anything as they got in line and Zach pushed them out to the parking lot and started loading up the trunk.

"My finger's going to be green in twenty-four hours." She grinned as she leaned against the side of the car, squeezing the two hearts together to make the ring stay on better.

"I know." He laughed. "I promise, I'll get you a real one when I come home."

"I like this one." Lindsey leaned over and kissed his cheek. "I'm going to keep it."

He stopped loading groceries to put his arms around her and kiss her again, soft this time, but full of something she knew he'd been holding back for a long time, and that sent a familiar feeling tingling through her body as she pressed herself back against him, wanting him, too. He nuzzled her neck, her ear, and whispered, "I'm going to keep *you*."

"Promise?" she teased.

"Yeah, I do." He kissed her again in response, deeper this time, longer. She gasped when they parted and he grinned. "So, now what do you want for graduation?"

"Nothing." She pressed her cheek against his chest, smiling across the parking lot and watching the young mother load her groceries and toddler into her car. "I have everything I want."

* * * *

"You're amazing!"

Lindsey blushed, nudging Zach with her bare knee as she typed away on his laptop. The phone rang, but Zach had it set to go straight to message. Lindsey frowned when she heard her mother's voice.

"Do you want me to get that?" he asked.

"No." She made a face at the phone. "Don't."

"I had no idea you could do that." He changed the subject, watching, incredulous, as she saved the spreadsheet she'd created so he could keep track of his new recruits.

"This is nothing." Lindsey snorted. "I used to hack into the school's computer mainframe all the time. When my stepdad started complaining about my grades, they suddenly got a lot better."

Zach raised his eyebrows, shaking his head. "If only I could get you to use your powers for good."

"But being bad can *feel* so good," she teased, closing the laptop and setting it on the coffee table before swinging her leg over to straddle him.

He groaned when she pulled her robe apart—that was new, too, red satin and short—to reveal she wasn't wearing anything underneath. The herbal baths Zach insisted she take after dinner every night had really helped heal her body much faster than she thought possible and her hair was still damp as she leaned in to kiss him. He tasted like the sweet ginger she'd used in the stir-fry she'd made for dinner.

"Let's be bad," she whispered, moving her hips in little circles, feeling him thickening through his jeans.

His hands moved under her robe, over the smooth expanse of her back, making her eyes close with pleasure. He'd touched her since—to bandage her, care for her—but they hadn't touched each other like this, and she had that desperate, hungry feeling in her belly.

"Are you sure you're ready for that?" His voice was controlled and cautious, but his eyes devoured the sight of her straddling his lap.

She took his hand and slid it between her thighs, kneeling up to give him better access. "More than ready, I think…"

He groaned as he slipped a finger between her smooth-shaved lips and Lindsey rocked her hips forward and back in response, sliding her pussy against his hand.

"I don't want to hurt you," he murmured as he slid a finger inside, making her gasp at the sweet sensation.

"You can't possibly." She leaned in, offering her breasts, and he closed his eyes and gave in, sucking gently at first one, then the other. The black and blue marks there had faded to pale yellow shadows, and the pink buds of her nipples grew cherry red and hard under the slow lash of his tongue.

But she couldn't take too much of that focused attention, and she slithered down between his thighs, unzipping his jeans and freeing his cock. He was rock hard, standing straight up, and he watched her through half-closed eyes as she worked her tongue around the head and down the shaft over and over, bathing him with her saliva.

"Come here," he murmured, tugging on her arm, but she didn't want to break the suction on his cock, swallowing almost half of him. When she resisted, he reached down and grabbed her hips, pulling her horizontal beside him on the sofa so he could reach underneath her, tweaking her nipples as she slid him further and further into her throat. The size of him made her gag, but she persisted, hungry and eager.

"Don't choke, baby," he urged, his breath coming faster as she worked between his legs, her hair falling in a silken cascade over his thighs.

"I like it," she gasped, giving up her mission only momentarily.

He groaned as she resumed her furious pace, her hand cupping the heavy weight of his balls, massaging gently, feeling them getting tighter and tighter as he groaned in pleasure. His hand slipped further down her belly, finding her clit and rubbing it, first back and forth, then round and round, her hips involuntarily following the same motion.

"Ahhhh god, baby, you're gonna—"

Lindsey squeezed the head of his cock—hard—coming up for air and admiring the shiny wet swollen head, nearly purple in color now, a product of her hard work.

"Oh no you don't," she warned, climbing into his lap and rubbing the tip back and forth between her slit. He gasped, his eyes closing, his mouth tightening, lips pursed. "I want you in me."

"Wait," he murmured, shaking his head and grabbing her hips, sliding her further up so she was straddling his belly. "You do that now and it'll be over in seconds."

"I don't mind." She nuzzled his ear, gasping in surprise when he stood with her in his arms, stepping out of his jeans and boxers as he headed toward the bedroom.

"I mind," he said, kissing her onto the bed, his tongue following a quick, determined path down her belly before she could even get the words out to protest, his mouth covering her mound.

"Zach," she objected, trying to wiggle away, but his hands on her hips held her fast, his tongue moving in delicious circles against her clit, not teasing, going straight for her pleasure center, focusing there. Her hands pressed his, useless against his strength, at first trying to dislodge him, and then, as the sensation grew, grabbing at him, pulling, her hips rolling under the hungry caress of his tongue.

"Oh god, oh no," she whimpered as his hands moved from her hips to her breasts, his fingers nudging her nipples hard, his tongue unwavering. She tried to fight the feeling, writhing on the bed as if his actions were painful, and in a way, they were—surrendering herself to her own pleasure, to his attention, made her shudder in torment.

But eventually, he won out, and she resigned herself to the humbling and powerfully slick frenzy between her thighs, her nails digging into his arms as she gave him her climax, hips pumping, thighs trembling, her soft cries of pleasure betraying the sweet torture of her body. She was glad Zach took his time as her breathing returned to normal again, kissing her pussy lips, her thighs, his hands roaming the soft curves of her hips and belly and breasts—she didn't think she could look into his eyes again so soon.

But then he was there, on her, sliding into her, whispering, "Are you sure?" Her only response was to meet his first thrust with her own and she buried her face against his neck as he began to move. Nothing had prepared her, nothing could have. She'd never felt this way before, and while her panicked mind raced, her body inevitably responded, giving into the weight and drive and purpose of him.

"Zach," she whispered, wanting to ask him to stop, to never stop, afraid of what was coming, and aching for it at the same time. "Oh please…"

He slowed, his cock throbbing between her legs, and she squeezed him with her muscles, an encouragement, making him groan.

"Are you okay?" He searched her face for a sign, and she swallowed, fighting to keep it in, everything in, just nodding. His head cocked as he looked at her, and then he rolled, taking her with him, and she found herself straddling him in the middle of the bed. She could do this—her robe slid down over her shoulders, and then she went to work on the buttons on his shirt, spreading it so she could run her hands over the hard muscles of his chest and belly. When they were naked, she began to ride him, rocking forward and back at first, then rolling her hips, making him moan and grab her ass as she moved.

She hadn't counted on his hands spanning her little hips, his thumbs opening her pussy lips, trapping her clit between them as she fucked him faster and faster. The feeling was maddening, driving her to distraction, until she forget entirely about getting him off and focused solely on the hot friction between her legs as he strummed her clit.

"Come for me, baby," he said as she balanced herself with her hands splayed on his chest, feeling weak, lightheaded, unable to control herself or anything at all. "Come on, Lindsey. Give it to me."

She gasped, the heat between them too incredible to resist, and she gave him exactly what he wanted, shuddering with her orgasm, her thighs and pussy squeezing him, her hands balled into fists, still fighting, but there was no point anymore. Collapsing against his chest, she buried her face against the side of his sweat-slick neck, and he wrapped one arm around her waist, the other hand he used to grip her ass and guide himself into her.

"You feel so good," he groaned, his cock thrusting up, in, over and over. "God, you're so sweet, so good…" She shook her head, but hung on tight, taking him into her again and again. "Oh baby, I'm going to come so hard!"

She gasped as he thrust one last time, deep and hard, driving them both up off the bed with it. He held her to him so tightly she thought she might break, but she didn't care, clinging to him as he spilled himself completely into her. His cock pulsed between her thighs, and she squeezed him, making him shudder and growl and thrust again. He held on when she went to move, not letting her go, his hands moving over her back, through her hair, his breathing still harsh and ragged as he kissed her mouth, her cheek, her ear, the top of her head.

"Are you okay?" he asked again, trying to get her to lift her head so he could see her eyes. She shook her head, feeling the sobs welling, and knew she was going to be unable to stop them. Her quivering body gave her away before the wetness of her tears did, and Zach sat up, cradling her in his lap.

"Oh baby, I'm sorry, I'm so sorry," he murmured, sounding pained, and Lindsey took a deep, hitching breath, trying to speak, but she couldn't form words. "I didn't mean to hurt you. Damnit…"

Instead, she cupped his face in her hands and kissed him through her tears, her mouth slanting across his as if she could devour him. He searched her face when they parted and she laughed, she couldn't help it, laughed and cried at the same time.

"I'm fine," she gasped, wrapping her arms around his neck, settling deep into his lap as he pulled the covers over them. "You didn't hurt me. You didn't... I'm just... I'm..."

He kissed the top of her head as she was overcome with a deep sob again, and then she laughed through her tears, looking up at him with more bewilderment and love than she'd ever felt for anyone or anything, sounding incredulous as the words spilled out: "I'm happy."

He smiled softly, folding her against him completely. "That makes two of us."

* * * *

Lindsey's head was spinning, and she might not have even seen them if it hadn't been for the cell phone Zach had insisted on buying for her sounding its "Coldplay" ringtone from her purse. She was practically skipping, planning a big, special dinner, and how she was going to tell him about the job interview at the recruiting office—she'd gotten it, all thanks to him, she was sure, and his bragging about her computer skills—and her subsequent registration at ITT Tech, where she would learn, at least more officially, how to do what she longed to on computers.

Although she felt a little guilty about all the money Zach had spent on her since she moved in, at least now she had both the possibility and opportunity to start paying her own way. The thought was both exhilarating and scary she could barely contain it, and when the phone rang, she was sure it was Zach—who else had the number, after all?—and she was going to spill it all before she could make any more dreamy little plans.

She stopped on the street corner—the bus stop was just around it, anyway—and began to dig for the phone, letting people pass her as she searched. It stopped before she found it, and she swore, sifting through lipgloss and gum, hearing the sound indicating someone had left a message. She had her hand on the phone, finally, and that's when she looked up and saw him.

They were building a book store across the street, a big steel two-story deal, lots of girders and mortar, and the construction was in full swing. There, standing half-behind an expanse of bright orange netting meant to keep the public out, she was sure, was one of the men who had raped her—not the one she'd labeled Smooth, the one with the easy, fluid voice, but the other one, Gritty, the one who had, she remembered and actually gagged standing there on the street corner, come in her mouth that night.

He was wearing a hard hat and writing something on a clipboard, his face slightly in shadow, but she knew him, would have known him anywhere. Then Smooth appeared behind him, and they faced each other, talking. Lindsey thought she might faint as she pressed herself back against the brick of the store behind her, looking for something solid to hold her up.

When the phone rang again in her hand, which was still half-buried in her purse, she startled and yanked it out, looking at the display. It was Zach. Oh, thank God. She flipped it open, pressed the phone to her ear, and whispered, "They're right across the street."

"Lindsey? Hello?"

Her voice was choked as she shrank against the building, praying they wouldn't look over, wouldn't see her, but she seemed unable to move. "Zach, I saw them. Both of them. The men who...who..."

"Where are you?" He understood, she could tell.

"The corner of..." She glanced up to be sure. "Woodward and Ten. They're right across the street at the construction site. *Right now.* They're just standing there talking—"

"I'm going to hang up and call the police. There's a hardware store there on the corner, right?"

She looked behind her, seeing red brick, but she knew the area well enough—her back was against the outside wall of the hardware store. "Yeah."

"Go inside. Tell them someone was bothering you, and the police are on their way. I'll be there in fifteen minutes. The police will probably be there before me." He swore under his breath. "Do you hear me?"

"Yes," she agreed, inching her way around the corner toward the hardware store door, feeling her way for the entrance. She couldn't take her eyes off the two of them, both laughing at some joke now.

"Do exactly as I say," he insisted. "I'll call you back in two minutes."

The line went dead. She slipped into the store, heart beating hard, breathing too fast, and she took a cart just to steady herself as she walked. It was more like five minutes before he called her back—she'd already told the first cashier she came to, a young girl with spiky black hair and a coiled tattoo on her neck, whose mascara-rimmed eyes grew wider and wider as Lindsey talked until she finally ran to get her manager.

The older man was more helpful, leading Lindsey to the back office, offering her a seat, bottled water.

She accepted both, and was just taking a long drink when the phone rang again.

"Are you okay?"

"I'm in the store," she said, smiling at the concerned-looking manager, who kept taking his wireless glasses off and wiping them on his shirt. "They're nice. They let me wait in the office."

"Good." He sounded a little less tense. "I'm on my way. The police should be there in a few minutes. They're sending an unmarked car. It was in the area."

"Okay." The thought of talking to the police made her stomach lurch and she closed her eyes, swallowing hard. "What…what are we going to do?"

"You're going to tell them."

She whimpered. "I want to go home."

"I'll be there to get you. Just a few more minutes, baby. I promise."

"I feel like I'm falling." She did. The world was spinning.

"You'll want to put your head between your knees…" The man with the glasses looked concerned.

"It's okay," Zach said, his voice choked. "I'll catch you, remember?"

She looked up at the sound of someone in the doorway. "They're here."

"Tell them everything," he insisted.

"Okay." She looked at the man in uniform standing in the doorway and wondered if she could.

"I love you, Lindsey."

"I love you, too."

She looked up at the cop, opened her mouth, and told him everything.

It was from the back of the unmarked cruiser parked on the street that she identified them both. And a few moments later, Zach's car pulled up behind them. The cop was suspicious when Zach knocked on the driver's side window, but Lindsey's relieved, "Zach! Oh, thank God!" was enough to convince him that it was safe to roll it down.

"Let me out!" Lindsey pulled on the door handle, locked from the inside.

The cop got out to talk to Zach, but left her inside, and the longer they stood there, the more panicked she felt. When the door finally opened, she flew into Zach's arms and he held her tight as she trembled against him.

"Can we go home?" she whispered. "Can we go home now?"

"Yeah, he said we can go. Come on." He put her in the car and slid into the driver's side. Lindsey didn't talk on the way, letting him hold her hand while he drove with the other.

But there was a message on the machine when they got home that made Lindsey curl into a fetal ball on the couch.

"I can't," she wailed as Zach knelt beside her, brushing the hair out of her face. "I can't!"

"Yes you can."

She tried to imagine it—like every bad *Law and Order*, standing behind two-way glass, facing them, knowing they couldn't see you, but still…

"And you will. Come on."

She thought of Brian and the games she had played leading up to that night. He hadn't meant for it to happen that way, she knew it, but if she stood up and started pointing fingers, he would be in just as much trouble. That weighed on her, but the thought of the things she'd done, the way she'd dressed, acted, instigated, the men she'd let feel her up, fuck her, use her—she pulled the sofa pillow out from under her head and pressed it over her flushed face to hide it.

"You don't understand," she whispered, when Zach pulled the pillow away and made her face him. "It went all wrong that night, I know. It wasn't supposed to…be like that. But I…I…" She closed her eyes, unable to look into his. "I went there to meet them. I knew…I knew what could happen."

"Did you say no?" Zach asked quietly, and she felt his hand in her hair again, stroking gently.

She remembered, and knew she had, clearly and unequivocally. She'd told them no over and over, and it just made things worse instead of better.

"Yeah." She opened her eyes, looking at him through prisms. "But that doesn't mean I didn't deserve it. How many times had I said yes before that?"

"Don't." He shook his head. "I don't care if you said yes until the very last minute, and then decided you didn't want to. No means no. Period."

She laughed, a short, strangled cry. "But 'no' never meant 'no' before…"

"And why was that? Because no one ever listened to you when you said 'no,' did they?" He touched her cheek, his eyes pained. "Your stepfather didn't listen. All the men who took advantage of you didn't listen. Lindsey, baby, you've been saying 'no' all along. It's just that no one was willing to stop and listen to what you actually meant."

Everything in her went silent as she stared at him, the slow realization creeping like cold fingers up her spine. She wanted to deny it, but she couldn't. All that time, she'd been saying "No"—egging them on, sure, teasing them, trying her best to get herself or someone else hurt, she realized with a flush of shame—but she never once stopped saying, "No."

"Okay." She sat up on the couch, wiping her eyes, blinking back any more tears, and managed to give him a small, hard smile. "Let's go."

She was going and, not just this one time, but now and forever, "No" was going to really mean "No."

* * * *

"Ugh, did you have to make me eat waffles?" Lindsey held her stomach as they approached the pavilion. It was crowded with a sea of kids in black robes, but there were far many more parents and siblings, grandmothers and uncles. All she had was Zach—not that she was complaining.

"You wanted waffles!" Zach laughed, tugging at the tassel on her mortarboard—a blue and white thing with a gold "2008"—making it go askew.

"Yeah, well…now I feel sick." She straightened her cap with a frown.

"You're going to be fine." He kissed her cheek, pointing to a sign that read, 'Graduates' with an arrow pointing down a flight of stairs. "I guess that's for you."

"How will I find you after?" She clung to his hand, hesitating at the top of the stairs.

"I'll wait right by this sign." He kissed her again, properly this time, a slow, lingering heat filling her middle to replace the nausea. "Now go, before they start without you."

She went down the stairs and packed herself into the crowd, hoping to be invisible in the sea of black. There were nearly a thousand graduates—it shouldn't be that difficult, she reasoned. And after today, she would be free, one rite of passage into adulthood officially taken, and more to follow—including the job she'd started two days ago, and school, which wouldn't start for another two weeks for the summer session.

Finding a spot by the wall, she sat down and waited for the organization machine to take over. It would, eventually, and then this whole thing would be over. Until then, she was going to concentrate on not being sick. The waffles Zach had brought to her in bed had been thick and rich and beyond delicious, and the sex they'd had afterward had been even better, but now it weighed heavily in her middle.

The truth was, she didn't want Zach to leave, and it was only a few weeks away now, looming large. She couldn't picture being on her own, couldn't imagine life without him anymore. He thought she was afraid of Smooth and Gritty—Robert Barnes and Donald McMillan according to the police report the prosecutor had showed her during their meeting with him. And she was, a little—they were out on bail, after all, and the trial had been so far in the future, nearly a month after Zach was due home, in fact—but no one knew where she was now.

She was more afraid of herself, of what she might do while Zach was gone. And she didn't even want to think about that.

"Hey, Lindsey."

Startled out of her thoughts, she looked up to see Brian standing there in his graduation cap and gown. Speak of the devil, she thought, quickly standing.

"Hi." She returned his greeting, and they stood there, lost in the awkwardness.

He finally cleared his throat. "I just wanted to say I was sorry."

"Okay." She nodded, wondering what he knew, how much he'd found out.

"I talked to Ralph. Those guys…I heard they were arrested."

So he knew. "They raped me."

"So did I." His voice was barely a whisper, his eyes on the floor. "I didn't mean for it to be like that. I didn't know…"

She put her hand on his arm. "It was bad. I'm sorry, too."

"They're making me testify." He swallowed, still not looking at her. "They say they're not going to charge me with anything, but they want me to go to court anyway."

She'd done her best to protect him and was relieved to hear it. "It got out of hand. For both of us."

He breathed a sigh. "I'll say."

"Hey, they're making us line up." She pointed to the front of the breezeway, where their old chem teacher was directed them into two lines—boys on one side, girls on the other. A thousand students, and she ended up next to Brian, filing two-by-two into the pavilion where family and friends were waiting to cheer as they walked across the stage to accept their respective diplomas.

He reached for and squeezed her hand just before they went out. "Happy graduation."

"You too."

She stepped out into the sunlight, already looking for Zach, and hoped, more than anything, that they'd both get some sort of happy ending after all.

* * * *

"I just want you to think about it." Zach dug into his pocket for his keys as Lindsey unzipped her black graduation gown—it was incredibly hot and itchy, and she'd barely made it home without stripping it off in the car.

"I don't need to think about it." She slipped the gown off over the jeans and t-shirt she was wearing underneath.

"I get that you're not ready to talk to her…"

Lindsey picked up the puddle of black material as Zach slid the key into the apartment lock, remembering the look on her mother's face in the pavilion. She'd found them just as Lindsey met Zach under the 'Graduates' sign, coming forward with congratulations and apologies and explanations. *Excuses, more like it*, Lindsey thought bitterly.

"She said she didn't know," Zach said, pushing the door open.

Lindsey snorted. "Bullshit. If I had a daughter who was doing what I was, I'd have suspected *something* was wrong."

"I guess I can't argue with you there." He sighed.

So she said she didn't know, Lindsey thought, tossing her cap and gown on the sofa. Her mother had found her journals, she'd said, and kicked her stepfather to the curb almost immediately. *A little too late*, Lindsey snorted to herself, not believing it was going to last for a minute. He'd be back, she was sure. Her mother couldn't possibly live on her own for too long.

It was the thing she'd always hoped for, desperately wished for, and yet now that it had happened, it didn't matter at all. She swallowed past the bitter irony of that thought as Zach put his arms around her from behind.

"When you're ready." He nuzzled her hair out of the way to kiss her neck. "Maybe you could just talk to her?"

She shrugged and, for his benefit, said, "I guess. Maybe."

"So are you ready for your gift?"

She could feel him grinning already.

"What do you have up your sleeve now?"

But he didn't have to tell her. Their voices had carried into the kitchen, and now a succession of short, plaintive yelps gave away his secret. Her eyes widened as she turned in his arms, her jaw dropping.

"You didn't!"

He was definitely grinning. "I did."

She squealed and took off running, stopping short at the baby gate now slung across the kitchen door where a black Labrador puppy scrabbled on the linoleum, jumping up as they approached, a little black nose nudging Lindsey's hand as she reached down to pet him.

"How did you do this?" She leaned down to pick up the puppy, who lapped happily at her face as she lifted him—yep, it was definitely a "he", she noted. There'd been no sign of a puppy when they left that morning.

"I had Nate drop him off." Zach scratched the wiggly black bundle of fur behind the ears, still grinning. Lindsey laughed, remembering how Nate had looked at her the first time she'd met him at the office just a few days ago, like he was keeping some sort of secret.

"What's his name?" she asked, giggling as the puppy squirmed in her arms, his pink tongue making the rounds of her face some more.

"Argyle."

She looked up at him and smiled, shaking her head. "Will I ever find a man who pays more attention to me than you do?"

"I doubt it, baby." He wrapped them both up in his arms, dipping his head down to hers to share in an exuberant puppy tongue bath. "I seriously doubt it."

Chapter Ten

If Lindsey had known how good puppies were at licking up tears and giving much-needed comfort, she would have found a way to get one years ago. Nuzzling Argyle's little belly with her cheek, she pulled the comforter up over both of them. The bed was too big now. She considered, for a moment, sleeping on the couch, but couldn't bear to be away from Zach's pillow—it still smelled like him.

That made her sob harder, and the puppy whimpered in sympathy, getting back to work on licking up the salt on her cheeks. The more she thought about those last moments with him, the harder she cried, but she couldn't seem to stop. The memory was too fresh for her to cut it off—just hours old, the apartment still lingering with his presence, his duffle packed, his uniform blinding white perfection over his muscled frame as he stood at the door, arms around her, both of them silent, the only sound Argyle clamoring at their heels.

"I can drive you," she said again, but he shook his head.

"Nate's my ride. Besides, I don't want to remember you waving goodbye at the airport. And I don't want you to have to drive home."

She'd proudly made it that far without tears, but they broke in a flood then, her chin quivering with their force. "I'd be a basket-case."

"I know."

The knock at the door startled them both. Zach swore under his breath, pulling her into him and kissing her, the memory of their marathon bedroom session over the weekend still fresh. But she wasn't thinking about how incredibly good their sex was—and it was—instead, it was all about loving him, and the hole in her heart he would be leaving when he walked out the door. She gave all of herself to him in that kiss, willing herself not to think about the possibility that it might be their last and yet acting as if it just might be.

It was the tears in his eyes as they parted that undid her entirely as he whispered, "I love you." She didn't even have the voice to return the words as he picked up his duffle and opened the door, going out quickly without a look back. Argyle yapped at the door after him, until Lindsey collapsed onto the floor, her whole body shaking with her sobs. Then the little black puppy joined the competition and whined and howled right along with her, and she didn't know who was louder.

She'd made it to the bed, she remembered. She wanted to be as close as possible to the last place they'd been happy together, aware of what was coming, but pushing it off as long as possible. And now...

Now life had to go on without him. She fingered the ring on a chain around her neck—the grocery store ring, which had, indeed, turned her finger green within twenty-four hours. She'd found a chain for it instead, and wouldn't take it off.

How could she possibly manage her life without Zach? She closed her eyes against the thought. She didn't know how, exactly, she was going to do it, but there was work, and school, and there was Argyle to take care of. She hugged him close, glad for the warmth and comfort, knowing he needed her as much as she needed him.

* * * *

After that first week of not eating, forcing herself out of bed, going through the motions, things started to fall into a routine she could live with. It went on that way for a month, at least, work, school, she and Argyle curled up on the couch, sharing Moo Goo Gai Pan out of the carton. She couldn't imagine that Puppy Chow was anywhere near the complete nutrition they claimed. And there was a phone call from Zach—just one—before they went under, he said. After that, there would be no contact at all until he was ready to come home.

That, actually, set her back another week, the sound of his voice, the sharp pain in her chest that immediately returned from its usual dull ache. But it was beyond good to talk to him, to whisper what she wanted to do to him—she could hear him squirming, and wondered afterward if their call was monitored, and laughed at the thought. She let Argyle lick the phone and bark at it to say hello, and she told him about her teachers, her classes, how Nate had followed Zach's instructions quite seriously and was "keeping an eye on her," stopping by once a week to check in.

She almost didn't tell him about her mother—she'd started calling every so often, leaving messages on Zach's answering machine. Lindsey's voice wasn't on it, but somehow her mother had gotten the number and knew she was living there. She just erased them, but she did break down and tell him about the calls.

"When you're ready," was all he said. She rolled her eyes and changed the subject.

It was that phone call, really, that pushed her into his closets, going through his things, looking over her shoulder as if he could walk in at any moment. God, she wished he would. She just wanted to find every piece of him she could, and was surprised at the little keepsakes, pictures of his high school graduation—a younger, grinning version of Zach looked at the camera, his arm around a woman who must have been his mother. God, she'd never even met his parents. Hadn't even asked…

Who was the little boy in the next photo? Was that Zach? She smiled at his camera-grin. Here was the same little boy playing in the sandbox with a little girl with cornrows. Who was she?

God, they knew so little about each other, she thought, sifting through a box of photographs, her heart aching with the knowledge. Things had happened so fast. Maybe too fast. A picture of a woman on the beach caught her attention—she was stunning, her skin like fine cocoa against the stark white of her bikini. She was looking over her shoulder at the camera, laughing. Lindsey turned it over and read the back: *Alicia, the Keys, 2007.* Just a year ago.

And she remembered the name. Of course she did. She could still hear the woman's voice on the answering machine: "Hey, baby, it's Alicia. I'm in town for a few days, and I'd *love* to get together…"

Did they? She wondered. The thought stabbed at her heart like a knife and she dropped the photo back into the box as if it were on fire, shoving it back into the closet. Argyle, who had been way too quiet behind her, had found one of Zach's shoes and was busily chewing the laces.

"No!" Lindsey reprimanded, snatching it away. "Bad boy!"

The puppy cowered, whining at her tone. She sighed, picking him up and apologizing with kisses. "Let's go for a walk, huh?"

She needed to get out and clear her head.

* * * *

Alicia called just after she'd sworn to Argyle that she wasn't going to snoop anymore. Her mother had just called, and Lindsey was sure it was her again and turned up the volume on the episode of *Desperate Housewives* she was watching, wanting to drown out the sound. Instead, the voice that came from the machine was much younger, and the call was most definitely not for her.

"Hi baby, it's Alicia. Can you give me a call back? You've got my cell number, right? I'll give it to you just in case..."

Lindsey stared in the direction of the voice, listening to the woman rattle off a phone number. She got up from the sofa in slow motion, going over to the machine and staring at the blinking red light. Her mother's message was on there—something about getting together and talking. She knew well enough how to erase them. One click would do it.

But now Alicia's number was on the machine. Did Zach have it? Probably. Of course, he was nowhere near a phone. And Lindsey knew, if she wrote it down, "just in case," it would sit like a growing temptation, and she would eventually break down and call it herself. She imagined the conversation that would ensue: "So, how do you know Zach? Is that so? How long did you go out?"

She snarled at the machine and stabbed the erase button, pressing it hard until it beeped. "You have no new messages," the voice said.

Good. That was better. That, she could live with.

* * * *

The tree fort looked exactly the same.

In some strange, convoluted way, it was the piling up of phone calls, from her mother, Zach, Alicia, that pushed her there, as if the world was turning backwards and she was traveling back in time. She wasn't wearing her shorts—they were locked up in some cabinet as evidence, awaiting the upcoming trial—but she'd found a bag of her old clothes in the closet when she was going through Zach's things, and a pair of Daisy Duke cut-offs and a black tube top had completed her transformation.

She didn't take Argyle. She didn't think he could walk so far. Instead, she drove the Camaro and parked it down the street, walking past her mother's house, trying to ignore the way her belly trembled as she drew nearer. Her stepfather's car wasn't there. Neither was her mother's. The house looked the same, though, the same as it had for years. It was the place she'd grown up, where she had fallen and been picked up by her father, the place she had traveled to the moon and back, until her daddy wasn't there anymore, and everyone forgot about her after that.

Her mother had forgotten her. Lindsey stood there, hugging her arms over her chest, thinking about Zach. What would she do if he never came home? How broken must her mother have felt after her husband hadn't returned from the Gulf War where the causalities were so negligible people didn't even think of it as a war? She shivered, shaking her head, and started walking again. She didn't want to think about it.

Somehow her feet followed themselves to the tree fort, and she found herself slipping out of her sandals to climb the rough boards up the side, settling herself in the very center. The height had never made her dizzy before, but it did now, and she didn't want to be too close to the edge. Not anymore. The day had been warm, but it was cooling toward evening now, the air crisp and clean, the leaves rustling softly around her.

She had brief flashes of memory—Brian and Ralph and that other kid, what was his name? She couldn't remember. So different from the night just a few weeks later, when she'd been beaten, raped, and she knew, if things had gone as far as they'd been ratcheting up to, she might have been dead.

Somehow, up until then, she'd felt like she was the one in control. She liked it rough, she wanted them to use her, she wanted them to… didn't she? She heard Zach's voice in her head.

You were saying no along.

Was it true? She didn't know.

"Hey, look who's here!"

She gasped and turned at the sound of the familiar voice, seeing him coming up the makeshift ladder, carrying a brown paper bag. "Ralph!"

"I haven't seen you in ages. Where've you been hiding?" He leaned back against the railing, getting comfortable and dropping a wink in her direction.

"Around." She tried to ignore the hammering of her heart, glancing toward the ladder. "Actually, I've got to get going…"

"Awwww, come on." He nudged her hip with his tennis shoe. "Stick around. We can have some fun." Pulling a bottle out of the bag, he uncapped it, taking a long swig of the amber fluid. He offered it to her, but she shook her head.

"Thanks anyway." Lindsey edged her way across the platform past him. He didn't make a move toward her, and she was grateful for that. "I'll leave you to it."

"Suit yourself." He shrugged as she swung her legs over the side.

She didn't answer him, and she willed herself not to hurry as she felt her way down the tree, rung by rung, slow and deliberate. When she reached the bottom, she looked up, and saw him peering over the side at her.

"Maybe some other time," he said with a grin.

"Bye." She gave him a quick wave, turning and heading down the path. She couldn't help looking over her shoulder once to see if he was following, but she didn't see any sign of him, and she hurried faster toward the car.

* * * *

"Where have you been?" Lindsey pulled the door open, expecting Nate. He had a habit of coming by on Sunday nights, and they'd started walking to the Dairy Queen on the corner. He always got a strawberry sundae, and Lindsey would get a small bowl of "doggie" ice cream for Argyle—they even put a milk bone in it—but she was much more choosy, changing her flavor choice from week to week. "I'm dying for a caramel…"

She wasn't expecting Ralph, and it was a nasty jolt to realize he knew where she lived. *He followed me*, she thought, as he leaned against the doorway and grinned. She could smell the Jack Daniels on his breath. Had he drunk the whole fifth by himself?

"What are you doing here?" The door wouldn't close. He was too far in already, and Lindsey wished Argyle were out of his little cage-house instead of sound asleep, so she'd have an excuse to shut it immediately.

"I followed you." Well, at least she'd been right about that. "Nice place."

"You can't be here." She tried to make her voice firm, resolute.

"Oh come on." Ralph's grin broadened as he stepped past her into the apartment. Her heart dropped as he stood there, looking around for a moment, and then glanced back at her. "You came out to the tree fort looking for it, and you know it." Reaching past her, he swung the door closed, stepping close and pressing her against the door's surface. "I just decided to make a house call."

She'd come home that evening after her little trip down memory lane—this really was home now—and had taken a long shower. Then she shoved the cutoffs, all her old clothes, back into the plastic bag, tied it up and wrote "Goodwill" in black Sharpie on the side. She was done with it. There was no going back, and even if the future with Zach was uncertain and more than a little scary, it was much more promising than what she'd put herself and everyone else through in the past.

"You don't know anything." She tried to reach behind her to the doorknob but he caught her wrist, squeezing hard. "Now, please leave."

His eyes narrowed. "I know a lot more than you think."

"What's that supposed to mean?" She couldn't shake him loose, and now he had her other wrist, both of them pinned behind her back.

"You know were asking for it that night, too," he sneered. "Just like every other time. Girls like you are all the same."

She repeated her request, struggling to remain calm. "You need to leave."

"Not 'til I get what I came for." He shoved his thigh between hers, his mouth crushing down, his tongue swirling, making her want to gag, and she did, turning her head, choking. "What happened, baby? You were so hot for it before."

"No," she gasped as he transferred his grip on both of her wrists to one hand, using his other to work his belt buckle. "I said no! Get out!"

"I know you don't mean that," he crooned, rocking the bulge of his cock through his jeans into her crotch as he loosened his belt. "Come on, baby, you suck it so good…"

"I said GET OUT!" Her voice rose to a scream, and the thought maybe the neighbors might hear—Mrs. Carmen next door, or Don from downstairs—made her even louder. "Help! Rape!"

"It ain't rape when I know you want it, baby." Ralph laughed, cupping the crotch of her jeans in his hand and rubbing hard.

"Stop it!" She struggled in his grip, but he was leaning against her, too heavy. "Don't. I said no!" She actually managed to break free for a moment when his hand moved to his jeans, reaching in to free his cock, and she ran straight to the phone, but didn't quite make it. He tackled her on the sofa, knocking the wind out of her with his weight.

"Hold fucking still!" he grunted, working the button her jeans. "I know you like it rough, but jeez…"

"I'm not playing!" Lindsey struggled, and realized she always struggled, didn't she? She always said no, didn't she? Why would he think she meant it this time? "I don't want to do this!"

The knock on the door made them both startle, and Ralph didn't think fast enough. His hand came down over her mouth just after she screamed out, "Come in!"

Nate's big frame filled the doorway, his eyes taking in the scene. "Need some help, Linds?"

Ralph stood quickly, buckling his pants, grinning. "We were just having a little fun. Sorry man, I didn't know she was with you."

Nate opened his mouth to say something, but Lindsey cut him off. "He was just leaving." She pointed to the door, noticing the tremble in her hand. "Right, Ralph?"

"Right, right." He edged toward the door, his eyes on the big guy standing there.

"Let him go, Nate," Lindsey insisted.

"Are you sure?" Nate frowned, looking between them. She nodded, and he stepped aside. She'd never seen anyone move quite so quickly as Ralph skittered by him and she heard him clattering down the stairs.

"Are you okay?" Nate shut the door and came to sit beside her. "Can I do anything?"

She looked up from where she had her head resting in her hands and gave him a weak smile. "I could use a hug."

He held out his arms, and she went to them for nothing but comfort, and he gave it to her. Tears stung her eyes but she willed them not to fall. "I want Zach."

"I know." He sighed. "I'm sorry."

Argyle barked from his cage, woken by the commotion, and Lindsey stood to go get him. "Let's go for some ice cream."

"You still up for that?" Nate asked, watching her take the puppy out and nuzzle him. He was getting big already.

"Yeah." She kissed Argyle on the nose and bent to pick up his leash from the coffee table and hook him up. "I could use a little sweetness right about now."

* * * *

"I'm coming home."

The words she'd been waiting to hear. She couldn't even speak at first, struggling with the closure in her throat, the happy tears. "When?"

"Two weeks."

"Oh thank god." She sat down on the sofa and Argyle jumped into her lap, barking at the phone like he wanted to talk, too. "I've missed you so much."

She couldn't believe it was over. Summer session had ended, and fall was starting again in just a few weeks. It felt like he'd been gone forever, and she felt just like a puppy, her whole body waggling in excitement at the thought of his homecoming.

"I'll meet you at the airport," she insisted, grabbing a pad and pen. "What flight?"

He told her and she wrote it carefully in big, fat letters, drawing a heart around the magical number.

"I can't talk long," he told her. "We're stateside now, though, so I can call you."

Phone calls! Two weeks of phone calls, and then he'd be home.

"Speaking of phone calls…" She swallowed hard, thinking, *why are you doing this?* But she had to know. Part of her had to know.

"Let me guess, your mother called?"

She frowned. "Well yeah, like every week, but that isn't what I was going to say."

"Are you ready yet?"

She blinked at the receiver. "I…I don't know." She'd been very good at avoiding them. The erase button on the machine got a lot of use. She never really even listened to the messages anymore, to what her mother was actually saying.

"So who else called that was so important?" he asked, changing the subject. She could hear him smiling, pictured it, and it filled her with a bright feeling of joy. "Was it the IRS?"

"No," she snorted. Then it was quiet again, and she hesitated. Did she really want to know? Did she? "I was wondering...who's Alicia?"

The silence stretched, and then he laughed. The sound made her feel both elated and ashamed for asking all at once. "Let me guess—you think she's some ex-girlfriend of mine?"

"Well..." Lindsey frowned, indignant. "It's not an illogical conclusion."

"She's my sister."

Her relief was worth the embarrassment. "I didn't know you had a sister."

"Yep." He chuckled. "Just the one. Were you jealous?"

"Shut up," she said, sticking her tongue out at the phone. "You'd be jealous, too."

"I am, baby." He sighed. "But you're mine now, and that's all that matters."

"I know." She smiled happily, leaning back on the sofa and letting Argyle curl up beside her. That one night with Ralph had proved it to her, if nothing else had. She didn't want anyone else but Zach, not anymore. But she wouldn't tell him about what had happened, she decided. She'd already sworn Nate to secrecy—he hadn't been happy about it, but they'd become close enough as friends to reluctantly agree that it was her choice—and she didn't want to hurt Zach anymore. He didn't need to know about her brief trip back, her flirting with disaster one last time.

What mattered was that she was sure now. She wouldn't ever be the girl she'd been before.

"So, now that we have that drama cleared up, are you going to call your mother?"

She rolled her eyes. "Don't you ever give up?"

"I wouldn't have you if I did."

She smiled, knowing already that it was going to be the longest and shortest five minutes of her life, her phone call with him, and it was. When she hung up, she sat with the cordless in her hand for a long time, just staring at it and thinking while Argyle slept next to her on the couch.

Finally, she began to dial the number of the place she used to call home.

Epilogue

"I've got a surprise for you," he whispered in her ear. She'd held onto him so long standing there with his duffle at their feet that already her arms ached but she still didn't want to let him go. Passengers jostled around them, calling to one another, many in a hurry to catch another flight, but they were both oblivious.

"Oh my god."

She looked around in panic as Zach got down on one knee in the middle of the airport, taking a small black velvet covered box out of his pocket.

He grinned. "You said that last time."

"What are you doing?" she hissed, trying to pull him up as passengers continued to file around them.

"What does it look like I'm doing?" He opened the box, his eyes on hers, looking for a reaction. "It's called a proposal."

"Zach…" Her eyes filled with tears and she wiped at them as they fell.

"Will you marry me?" The hand that held the box shook. "For real this time?"

"It was always real," she whispered, fingering the lid to the box, not quite ready to touch the actual ring. "I was afraid to believe it, but it always was."

He smiled, holding the box up higher, an offering. "Will you?"

She squealed and said, "Yes!" The ring was beautiful, huge and a perfect fit as he slid it on. He stood to take her in his arms, their kiss sealing the deal, and she gasped when they parted, whispering in his ear, "I have a surprise for you, too."

"Oh?"

She was wearing a jacket, although it wasn't that cool outside, even for September, and she unzipped it slowly, opening it to reveal her secret. Puzzled, he stared for a moment, and then his eyes widened, coming up to meet hers.

"I thought…?"

"I don't know." She shrugged, just as bewildered, but never more happy.

And then he was on his knees again, his arms wrapped around her waist, kissing the rounded bump of her stomach over and over where their child was growing.

"You win," he grinned, standing and pulling her into his arms, and swinging her around. She squealed, laughing. "You had the bigger surprise."

"Stop!" she gasped, still giggling. "You're making me dizzy!"

"It's okay." But he did, putting her down and kissing her, his mouth full of longing and tenderness and promise. His words were whispered, just for her, "I'll always catch you, remember?"

How could I forget? She smiled and pressed her ear to his heart, relishing the strong, steady beat there, the solid feel of him against her. She didn't speak her response out loud, not there in the middle of the airport, but she knew he felt it.

And more importantly, she knew he meant what he said. He was willing to wait, willing to be patient while she learned to walk instead of crawl. *Maybe,* she thought with a smile as he kissed her again, feeling herself floating with him somewhere else away from everyone and everything…*maybe, even, to fly.*

And it didn't matter if she fell.

He really would be there to catch her.

Selena Kitt is a bestselling and award-winning author of erotic and romance fiction. She is one of the highest selling erotic writers in the business with over a million books sold!

Her writing embodies everything from the spicy to the scandalous, but watch out-this kitty also has sharp claws and her stories often include intriguing edges and twists that take readers to new, thought-provoking depths.

When she's not pawing away at her keyboard, Selena runs an innovative publishing company (excessica.com) and in her spare time, she devotes herself to her family—a husband and four children—and her growing organic garden. She does bellydancing and photography, and she loves four poster beds, tattoos, voyeurism, blindfolds, velvet, baby oil, the smell of leather, and playing kitty cat.

Her books EcoErotica (2009), The Real Mother Goose (2010) and Heidi and the Kaiser (2011) were all Epic Award Finalists. Her only gay male romance, Second Chance, won the Epic Award in Erotica in 2011. Her story, Connections, was one of the runners-up for the 2006 Rauxa Prize, given annually to an erotic short story of "exceptional literary quality," out of over 1,000 nominees, where awards are judged by a select jury and all entries are read "blind" (without author's name available.)

She can be reached on her website at www.selenakitt.com

FORBIDDEN FRUIT
By Selena Kitt

Leah and Erica have been best friends and have gone to the same Catholic school since just about forever. Leah spends so much time with the Nolans—just Erica and her handsome father now, since Erica's mother died—that she's practically part of the family. When the girls find something naughty under Mr. Nolan's bed, their strict, repressive upbringing makes it all the more exciting as they begin their sexual experimentation. Leah's exploration presses deeper, and eventually she finds herself in love for the first time, torn between her best friend and her best friend's father.

NOTE TO READERS: This story appeared in another, now rather infamous book of mine (UNDER MR. NOLAN'S BED). This tale was previously released as

Plaid Skirt Confessions and is a slightly less naughty, but no less sexy re-telling of those events--updated and redressed for your reading pleasure with an ending that may leave you a little more satisfied.

Warnings: This title contains erotic situations, lesbian sex, sex toys, and also makes mention of pornography, salmon, amusement parks, chocolate covered strawberries, brownies (as well as girl scouts), plaid skirts, naughty uses for confessionals and some sacrilegious humor.

EXCERPT from <u>FORBIDDEN FRUIT</u>:

Erica fell fast asleep that night, but I rolled around on the floor in the sleeping bag, desperately wanting to know if Lucy's wacky plan had really worked. I hadn't heard them come up—at least, I thought I hadn't. But I couldn't hear them downstairs anymore either. There was no more music, no more throaty laugh.

Had she gone home? Were they sleeping in his bed? The thought made my hands curl into fists, my nails digging into my palms. Finally I couldn't stand it. I got up and crept toward the bathroom. There was no light in his room. That was a good sign—I hoped.

I turned the bathroom doorknob, easing the door open and reaching for the other door—the one that led to his room. I had to know. I didn't care if she was there, I just had to know. Okay, that was a lie, I cared, way too much, and I could feel how much in the way my heart pounded in my chest as I turned the knob.

"I'm not in there," Mr. Nolan whispered, stepping out of the darkness and putting his arm around my waist, pulling me away from the door. I would have screamed in surprise, but his hand went over my mouth. "But that's not what you want to know, is it?"

I gasped, whirling around in his arms. He must have been sitting on the edge of the tub in the darkness, I reasoned, my heart hammering in my chest.

"What are you doing?" I hissed as he shut the door quietly and turned on the nightlight over the sink.

"Waiting for you."

I leaned back against the counter, staring up at him. I could see the truth of it on his face, raw and even painful.

"Did she go home?" I whispered, conscious of Erica sleeping in the other room.

He swallowed and shook his head. His eyes were pleading with me, trying to tell me something, but I couldn't understand. "No. She's sleeping in my bed."

"Why?" I felt tears stinging my eyes and I willed them not to fall. "What did I do?"

He sighed, closing his eyes and running a hand through his hair. "Oh Leah. Nothing. Everything. I don't know."

"Do you really like her?" I whispered, blinking fast and taking a step toward him. He didn't move back, and we were almost belly to belly. "Is she…is she what you want?"

He opened his eyes and looked down at me, arms hanging at his sides, head down. He looked defeated. "No."

"Then why?" I hissed, shoving at his chest with the flat of my palm. "You asked her out again! You cooked her dinner! You *slept with her!* Why?"

"I don't know!" He shook his head. "Why did you do what you did? Putting the magazines and videos on my bed? Was it supposed to scare her off?"

I sighed, crossing my arms. "That was Erica's idea, not mine."

"Erica?" He frowned.

I shrugged, acting like I didn't care if he believed me. "This isn't fair."

"No," he admitted, moving forward a little, lifting my chin. "It's really not."

"I just want to know why." I met his eyes. I felt my chin quivering in his hand and tried to stop it, but I couldn't. "Please just tell me why."

"You want to know why?" His eyes flashed in the dimness, moving over my face. "Fine, I'll tell you why. For the same reason I was sitting here at one in the morning, waiting for you."

I stared up at him, eyes wide.

He shook his head, looking pained. "I can't stop thinking about you, Leah. Everywhere I go, everything I do, there you are. I can't get you out of my head."

My throat and chest tightened at his words and I nodded. I knew exactly how he felt.

"I thought…" He swallowed, his hand moving down my neck, over my shoulder, his gaze following the curve there. "I thought that if I moved on, I could stop this crazy thinking. This feeling I have for you…"

"What feeling?" I pressed against him. "Tell me."

"Leah…" He whispered my name, using his thumb to rub over my lips. "I took her to bed tonight, yes, I did. I fucked her senseless, until I couldn't see straight—" His words shot arrows into my heart and I felt the sting of them in my chest. "And every time I closed my eyes, I saw your face." He pressed me back toward the counter with the weight of his body. "It wasn't her I was touching or kissing or fucking—it was you, Leah. Every minute I was with her, I was wishing it was you."

"Oh god." I reached up and put my arms around his neck and pulled his mouth down to mine.

It was like sinking into something dark and warm and soft, the safest place I'd ever been.

YOU'VE REACHED
"THE END!"

BUY THIS AND MORE
TITLES AT
www.eXcessica.com

eXcessica's YAHOO
GROUP
groups.yahoo.com/
group/eXcessica/

Check us out for updates
about eXcessica books!

Made in the USA
Middletown, DE
28 November 2020